Waltham Forest Libraries (H)

Please return this item by the last date stamped. The loan may be renewed unless required by another customer.

Dec 21		

D0533531

Need to renew your books?
http://www.walthamforest.gov.uk/libraries or
Dial 0333 370 4700 for Callpoint – our 24/7 automated telephone renewal line. You will need your library card number and your PIN. If you do not know your PIN, contact your local library.

Encore, encore!
LoveReading4Kids

Shortlisted for the Independent Bookshop Week Award.

The Runaways of Haddington Hall

Vivian French

WALKER
BOOKS

First published 2021 by Walker Books Ltd
87 Vauxhall Walk, London SE11 5HJ

2 4 6 8 10 9 7 5 3 1

Text © 2021 Vivian French

The right of Vivian French to be identified as the author of this work has
been asserted by her in accordance with the Copyright, Designs and Patents
Act 1988

This book has been typeset in Baskerville

Printed and bound by CPI Group (UK) Ltd, Croydon CR0 4YY

British Library Cataloguing in Publication Data:
a catalogue record for this book is available from the British Library

ISBN 978-1-4063-8753-7

www.walker.co.uk

For Isla,
with much love

One

"**Y**ESSSS!" MINNIE O'SULLIVAN GAVE A whoop of triumph as she tipped the last handful of grated soap flakes into the enormous copper washtub in front of her. The steam from the boiling water swirled around her head; on the other side of the tub, Mam was pushing a sodden mass of dirty washing round and round in the frothing suds.

Her mother nodded at her. "Good girl. What'd I do without you?" She pointed to the pile of logs in the corner. "See to the fire, there's a duck. Don't want it going out, do we?"

Taking her cue, Minnie stoked up the fire burning beneath the blackened copper boiler before going to the door and swinging it to and fro, encouraging the flames to leap and flare.

Perspiration trickled down her back, and her damp clothes clung to her; Mam's dress and apron were so wet, she looked as if she had been thoroughly boiled herself.

As the flames steadied, Minnie went to stand outside for a moment. The cold evening air was a blessed relief; she took several deep breaths before scuttling back into the wash house.

"Go outside a minute, Mam. Cools you down lovely!"

"Got to get this lot through the mangle first." Mam O'Sullivan picked up the wooden tongs and hauled the scalding sheets and shirts out of the copper, then dropped them into the large wooden tub of cold water alongside. "It's got to be done by tomorrow. If I'm late, they'll be back to Elsie Addams' wash house next time they've got a load. Now, give us a hand with Uncle Fred."

Minnie grinned. Uncle Fred was the name she and Mam had given to the enormous iron mangle that was kept at the back of the small, dark yard outside. It was old, and much given to bursting out in a rash of rust, and Minnie was convinced that it hated her. All the same, it saved an enormous amount of work as the wooden rollers squeezed nearly all the water out of the wet washing. It was Minnie's job to turn the heavy handle while Mam fed the washing through the rollers, and there was an art to this. If done carefully, the neatly folded sheets could be hung over the range to dry, and didn't need ironing.

With much heaving and shoving, they moved Uncle Fred into the wash house, and began the mangling. Minnie and her mother had done it so often that they had established a rhythm; Minnie burst into song as she turned the handle, and her mother joined in.

"Ring-a-ring o' roses, a pocket full of posies…" It was the song they always sang, and when it came to the sneezing, they enjoyed trying to out-sneeze each other.

"Mam, Mam! I had a dream – a monster did eat me all up."

The song and the mangling came to an abrupt stop. Minnie's little brother Bobby had got out of bed and come to find Mam, and was standing dangerously near the glowing embers beneath the copper tub.

Mam, her arms tangled in heavy wet sheets and shirts, froze. "Quick, Min, get him!"

Minnie let go of the mangle handle, and ran to grab Bobby and lift him away from danger.

"You're not allowed in here, Bobs," she scolded. "It's dangerous! You knows that."

Bobby began to cry. "I didn't do nothing..." He held out his arms. "See? The monster eated me all over!"

His arms were covered with angry red spots, and Mam sighed. "That's bedbugs, Bobby pet. Just bedbugs, that's all." With a heave, she extricated herself from the washing and squelched across the muddy brick floor to pick Bobby up and cuddle him. "There, there, my love. Mammy will find you a piece of bread, and tuck you up tight." She looked at Minnie over Bobby's curly head. "You didn't need to shout at him. He's only little."

As Mam stomped away, Minnie scowled at the mangle. It had been terror for her little brother that had made her snap at him, and she was angry that Mam hadn't understood. She gave the handle a vicious twist to relieve her feelings; the mangle responded with a dribble of water and an unpleasant ripping sound.

"Oh!" Minnie went pale. Nervously, she peered at the washing and yes: a sleeve had torn.

Minnie's heart fluttered, and her mouth went dry. Shirts were Mam O'Sullivan's pride and joy; she was famous for sending them back to their owners spotlessly white and crisply ironed. The possibility of damaging a shirt was spoken of with a hushed voice – it would ruin Mam's reputation … and now Minnie had done just that.

Hearing her mother's heavy footsteps returning, Minnie took a deep breath. "Mam … Mam, I've done something really bad." Her voice shook. "I gave the handle a turn, and it's torn something. I'm ever so, ever so sorry, Mam."

Mam O'Sullivan stared at her daughter. "What did you do that for?"

Minnie hung her head. "I was mad 'cos you told me off."

"Let's have a look." Mam studied the damage in silence before turning the handle backwards to release the shirt. "It ain't good, Min. Sleeve's half off at the shoulder. I'll have to pay for that."

"Pay?" Minnie was aghast.

Mam shrugged. "What did you expect, pet? Damaged, ain't it?"

Minnie swallowed. Her mother's weary accep-
tance was unusual, and worrying. Mam's temper
was like Minnie's: quick to flare up, and equally
quick to die down again.

"Aren't you mad at me?" she asked.

"I'm too danged tired to be mad, Minnie
love." Mam pushed her damp hair out of her
eyes, and put the torn shirt to one side. "If truth
be told, I'm tired to death of work-work-working
… and nothing to show for it but trouble."

"Oh, Mam." Minnie ran to hug her mother.
"Don't you fret about that shirt! I tore it so I'll go
to the Dog and Duck and tell them so, and say
how it wasn't nothing to do with you."

Mam put her huge arms round her daughter, and gave her a squeeze. "It's the gentry that
wears them kind of shirts, Min. They don't take
no notice of the likes of us."

Minnie tossed her head. "I don't care if it's the
queen of England. I'm going, and that's that."

Minnie woke up the following morning with
a niggling feeling that all was not right in her
world. Bobby was peacefully asleep beside her,
only occasionally stirring to scratch at his bites,

and Mam was snoring ferociously on the other side of the room. All of this was usual and familiar ... so what was wrong? They had finished the wash, and the smooth white sheets and shirts were draped over the wooden racks that hung from the ceiling. Minnie glanced up at them and wondered, as she had wondered a thousand times before, what sleeping in clean white linen would feel like.

Her eye was caught by the last shirt, and her stomach lurched. This was what was troubling her: not the torn sleeve, but Mam's weary response ... and her own promise to confess.

She looked across at her mother. Mam was lying on her back; her mouth was open, and her snores were echoing round the room. Studying her, Minnie saw how lined and worn her face looked in sleep.

Mam's getting old! she thought, and a cold hand twisted in her stomach. *Maybe I ought to look out for her more.*

Creeping out of bed, Minnie tiptoed across to the range. It was still alight, but only just, and when she reached up to feel the sheets, they were still damp.

She scrabbled in the bottom of the coal bucket, but it was empty. With a sigh, Minnie pulled on her clothes and her battered old boots and stomped to the door to fetch logs from the wash house. The sheets had to be bone dry before they were taken back to their owners, or there'd be complaints.

As Minnie coaxed the range back into life her mother heaved herself up from her bed.

"Good girl, Min," she said, and then, "No coal left?"

Minnie shook her head, and Mam sighed. "Got your boots on? Run down to Aunt Bet and see if she'll lend a bucketful. Tell her she'll get it back soon as the Dog and Duck's paid up. I'll never get them shirts ironed, otherwise."

Minnie opened her mouth to protest, then closed it again. Wasn't she meant to be looking out for Mam?

"I'll run all the way," she promised. Snatching up a shawl from the back of a chair, she wrapped it round her shoulders, blew Mam a kiss, and headed for the door.

Once outside, she began to whistle. There was a chill in the air, but the wind was light and the sky had patches of blue. Swinging the bucket, Minnie looked around her as she hurried out of the alley and down the street; she knew every one of the families squashed into the smoke-blackened houses that leaned towards each other as if apologizing for the lack of comfort inside.

Aunt Bet's rooms were in the end house, next to a piece of waste ground where she kept several scrawny chickens and grew vegetables. As Minnie pushed open the street door, a faint suggestion of cabbage and onion soup welcomed her in.

"Why, if it isn't our Min!" Aunt Bet greeted Minnie with a beaming smile. "Come in, love! Got time to help me with the eggs?"

Minnie, aware that her mother was waiting, shook her head. "Sorry, Aunt Bet. Mam sent me to ask for the borrow of a bucket of coal. It's the smoothing irons – they don't get hot enough on a wood fire, see. And we ain't got no coal left."

Aunt Bet sighed. "And there was me thinking you was here to save my poor old aching bones."

Minnie grinned. "I'll come another time. So, can Mam have the coal? She'll give it back, soon as she gets paid."

"Course you can, love." Aunt Bet pointed to the coal box in the corner. "Help yourself. Not too much, mind! And there's half a loaf of bread for you over there on the sideboard. Our Jeb, he's working for a baker – and he gets stale loaves by way of payment."

As Minnie staggered out of Aunt Bet's door and set off towards home, the heavy bucket of coal weighing down one arm and the half-loaf of bread tucked under the other, she was surprised to see a girl of her own age and an elegantly dressed middle-aged woman standing on the other side of the street.

The woman was holding up her skirts and looking down her nose at the state of the road, but the girl was looking eagerly about her as if she was in another country.

For a moment Minnie wondered if they were lost, and if she ought to help them – but the woman's arrogant expression decided her against making any such offer.

Whistling cheerfully, she took a firmer grip on the bucket handle and went on her way.

Two

THE TWO STRANGERS WATCHED HER GO, and the woman shook her head.

"Just listen to that girl, Edith. Whistling – whistling like a boy! Yet another shocking example of the complete lack of standards in the lower classes."

Edith, who had been thinking how happy the girl had sounded, tried to look concerned. "Oh yes, indeed, Mrs Haddington," she said. "Mother always says girls should never whistle."

Mrs Haddington was pleased. "Dear Lady Lavingley is a splendid example to us all. Listen to her, Edith dear, and learn. Now – take a look about you. You'll find this unfortunate area is swarming with children. I've seen them creeping and crawling around the back of the shops hunting for scraps of food, and they'll eat anything they find. This may be hard for you to believe, but I once saw a child snatch an old chewed bone from a dog. Horrible: simply horrible!"

Edith hesitated before answering. As an only child, she had led a sheltered life; her education had been in the hands of a governess who had been chosen for her elegant ankles, and who believed that as long as her pupil was allowed access to books, no further tuition was necessary. Recently the governess had walked away on her elegant ankles, and Edith's mother, delighted to save expense, had informed her daughter that her school days were now over. Works of charity, she suggested, would provide her with a useful occupation.

Having read a great deal about orphans and orphanages, Edith had joined the Literary Ladies' Charitable Association for Orphans with high expectations of spending time with apple-cheeked girls in scarlet flannel petticoats, who would greet her with smiling faces. Today was the first time she had met Mrs Haddington, the founding member of the charity, and so far, she had not been impressed. She had, however, been brought up to be polite.

After some thought she suggested, "Perhaps the child was hungry?"

Mrs Haddington bristled. "Really, Edith, where are your principles? It is never, never acceptable to take food from a poor dumb animal!"

Unable to think of an appropriate reply, Edith smiled faintly. "I wonder where that girl was taking the coal?"

"Don't wonder, Edith. Wondering is a waste of time, and time should never be wasted."

Mrs Haddington pulled a small notebook and a gold pencil from her purse.

"But she looks strong and reasonably healthy. She is certainly of interest to me. I shall make a note. Where are we? Oh yes. Pocket Street. I wish to show you the house in which we will educate and improve the lives of five carefully selected girls: two girls are already in residence – rescued from a most disreputable person who ran a disgusting old clothes shop." Mrs Haddington gave a theatrical shudder. "When we reach the house, you will meet them."

"Thank you," Edith said, and then, seeing that Mrs Haddington was expecting her to say more, added, "It sounds a very interesting project."

"It is." Mrs Haddington beamed. "We believe it is our duty to save these young women from ignorance, and provide them with skills that will allow them to lead God-fearing and respectable lives. They will be grateful to us for the remainder of their useful and hard-working existences."

"I'm sure they will," said Edith, but she did not sound convinced.

Her companion gave her a sharp look, then bustled Edith round the corner to where their carriage was waiting – detailing the many glories of the charitable association's house as they hurried along.

"Not only does each girl have her own bed to sleep in, but she also has a blanket. And we intend to provide them with identical yellow-and-black uniforms." Mrs Haddington was proud of her choice; should any girl be foolish enough to try and leave her new home, she would be easily identified by the wasp-like dresses. "Everything is made of the most hard-wearing materials. Self-adornment or decoration is to be frowned upon. These young women have no place in their lives for such things."

Edith suppressed a sigh as she seated herself in the carriage. Somehow, she was unable to imagine apple-cheeked girls in yellow-and-black dresses.

Arriving at their destination, Mrs Haddington opened the carriage door with a flourish. If she had noticed Edith's silence, she made no mention of it as she proudly pointed at a depressed-looking house squatting in a marshy garden enclosed by a broken-down wall.

The roof was sagging as if it had given up hope years before, and the two crooked chimneys leant towards each other in mutual dejection. The building was surrounded by such heavy trees that no ray of sun would ever be able to find its way through to cheer the inmates, and the few ailing plants that bordered the path drooped miserably.

"And here we have it: Haddington Hall! In this delightful residence five lives will be changed for ever. Come and meet the girls, and our housekeeper."

Edith followed the older woman through the creaking front door and into a narrow hallway. It was dark and damp, and smelt strongly of mould and mushrooms. Edith wrinkled up her nose, but Mrs Haddington looked round with a satisfied air.

"This must truly seem like paradise to our girls," she said. "Ah! Here's Mrs Krick."

A door had opened at the end of the hallway, and an elderly figure wrapped in a collection of shawls came shuffling out, accompanied by a large and ferocious mongrel. As soon as the dog saw Edith, it gave a low menacing growl, and Edith backed hastily away.

Mrs Krick gave a high pitched shriek of laughter. "Gobbler won't hurt you, Miss. Not unless he sees you running. Run away, and he'll have you by the ankle, quick as a wink."

"Is that a good thing?" Edith was disliking everything about Haddington Hall. Only the fear of appearing rude prevented her from gathering up her skirts and hurrying away. "Won't he frighten the girls?"

This time it was Mrs Haddington who laughed. "Of course he will! Mrs Krick's last post was at a very well-respected school for boys, and Gobbler was an invaluable asset. Not a single boy ever ran away, for fear of being bitten."

Edith said nothing. Her idea of philanthropy was of gracious women wearing floating robes, administering nourishing beef tea whilst soothing fevered brows with cool hands. A house that was dark and dank, and that smelt of mould and mushrooms, was as far from this vision as it was possible to be, and she hated it. Added to that, it appeared the girls were going to be imprisoned by a drooling dog, and receive no useful education whatsoever.

Mrs Haddington saw Edith's dubious expression, and began to bluster. "My dear Edith! I understood that you wished to be of assistance to me and my charitable cause, but I do wonder if your character is quite suitable. We believe in positivity, you see. *Positivity* and *practicality* are our watchwords." She reassured herself with a firm nod. "My carriage is outside. Would you prefer to leave us?"

Edith wanted nothing more than to leave; only the thought of how angry her mother would be if she came back early prevented her from accepting Mrs Haddington's invitation. Lady Lavingley expected her daughter to do as she was told.

"I'm sorry." Edith hoped she sounded sincere. "It's just that all this is very new to me. But you're quite right. I know nothing about these things."

Mrs Haddington immediately softened. She was secretly regretting her words: to lose an aristocratic connection on her first day would undoubtedly result in unpleasant gossip. She had, early that morning, sent several notes to dear friends and darling acquaintances, informing them that *Lady Lavingley, instead of merely sending a donation to our worthy cause, has done me the great honour of entrusting her precious daughter to my care.*

Now, in patronizing tones, she said, "You are very young, my dear. I accept your apology, and believe we will understand each other better from now on."

"Thank you." Edith bobbed a curtsy.

Mrs Haddington smiled her most gracious smile. "And now, let us meet Peg and Molly, our two residents. They're not sisters, but they're good friends. So delightful! Mrs Krick – would you be so kind as to call them?"

Mrs Krick looked sour. "I doubt they'll come, Ma'am. They've taken against the dog, and that's a fact. They don't come down except for meals, and the dog, he has to be locked away." She coughed. "May I ask, Ma'am – when is the young person you spoke of coming? The one who's going to look after the girls?"

"Nellie will be here tomorrow, Mrs Krick, before the two sisters arrive."

Mrs Haddington gave a dramatic sigh.

"Edith, my dear, you must remember to tell Lady Lavingley that I have asked my very own parlour maid to assist with my work here at Haddington Hall. A great sacrifice for me, of course, but she will teach our residents the skills they need."

Pleased, Edith said, "That sounds very generous of you. Does she like young people?"

Mrs Haddington hesitated. She had very little idea of what her maid liked or disliked, or indeed if she had any experience of anything other than dustpans and brushes. "Yes," she said firmly. "She dotes on children, and has an excellent character." Striding to the bottom of the stairs, she called, "Peg! Molly! Come down, my dears: I have someone here who wishes to meet you."

A door on the landing above opened, and a hoarse voice shouted, "We're not going nowhere if that dog's about, and we don't want to meet nobody! Prying nosy parkers, all of you." And the door slammed shut.

Edith was taken aback by this response. "Could the dog be put in the kitchen?" she suggested.

But Mrs Haddington was having second thoughts. It seemed the resident orphans were not as grateful as they should be. *I shall instruct Nellie to deal with that*, she thought, and turned to Edith.

"Perhaps today is not the day for introductions, dear. We'll take our leave for now."

Edith was not sorry. The small, dark rooms and pervasive smell of damp were making her feel distressed.

Mrs Haddington took her arm and escorted her to the waiting carriage. As she did so, she explained that Mrs Krick had a heart of gold, and that Nellie would be a second mother to the girls.

Edith decided to keep her own thoughts on the matter to herself – and as the carriage began to move, Mrs Haddington leant forward.

"My dear, this afternoon I am hosting a little fundraising tea party. Could your mother spare you, do you think?"

Edith was certain there would be no objection, and Mrs Haddington was delighted.

"You may, perhaps, meet our patron, the Reverend Obadiah Marpike ... such a charming man! And, I believe I can say, a very dear friend of mine."

Mrs Haddington blushed a ferocious shade of puce, and looked coy.

"He's also the treasurer of our charity: he works absolute wonders with our little pot of savings. And I can tell you in confidence, my dear, that he also looks after my personal financial affairs – and all out of the goodness of his heart!"

Edith was not particularly encouraged by this description. All the same, she was beginning to feel intrigued by the charity; it was all so very different from her expectations...

And any kind of tea party would make a change from the boredom of her day-to-day life with her mother.

Three

~~~

REACHING HOME, MINNIE FOUND HER mother sorting pillowcases and shirts into piles, while Bobby sat cross-legged on the bed sucking his thumb. When he saw the bread that Minnie was carrying, his eyes opened wide, and his peaky face broke into a huge smile.

"You got bread, Min!"

"Aunt Bet gave it me." Minnie tore off a crust and handed it to him. "Her Jeb's working for a baker."

As Bobby took the bread, Mam picked up the coal bucket. "Minnie pet, stack up the fire: we got work to do. If that bundle of washing ain't back at the Dog and Duck by five tonight we'll not get paid."

Pausing in front of the range, Minnie said, "You take some bread, Mam. You ain't had nothing yet today – and you slipped Bobby most of yesterday's pie. Don't go thinking I don't notice them little tricks you play!"

"Get any sharper and you'll cut yourself," Mam said. "I'll eat when I'm done." And she moved over to the pair of flat irons that were kept under a cloth to keep the dust away; taking them down, Mam handed them to Minnie to heat in front of the range. "Get them hot, Min, and get me a jug of clean water. The shirts will need damping down."

The mention of shirts made Minnie blush, and her mother gave her a sideways look. "Want to change your mind?"

"No." Minnie was firm. "I tore it, and I'll tell them."

By half past four in the afternoon, Mam O'Sullivan, red-faced and perspiring, had finished the ironing. The sheets were dry and folded, and everything was carefully packed in the large wicker basket belonging to the Dog and Duck.

"Get yourself ready, Min," Mam said. "Enry will be here any minute to collect. You going to go with him, then?"

All afternoon, a feeling of dread had been hanging over Minnie, and several times she had wished that she hadn't been so hasty in her decision to confess in person. She had never been to the Dog and Duck, and her imagination had begun to work overtime. Who would she see? Who did the shirt belong to? What would the owner say to her?

Mam, who had sunk onto a chair, laughed. "They won't eat you, Min!" Before she could say anything more, there was a knock on the door, and Minnie went to see who was there.

The knock was followed by the appearance of a large top hat, old and battered, above a threadbare jacket, ragged trousers and a pair of broken-down boots.

"Afternoon, Missus! Afternoon, Min! Wotcher, Bobs!" The hat was swept off, revealing a pale face with huge eyes and an enormous smile. "Got your basket ready?"

"All done." Mam greeted him cheerfully. "Still wearing that old hat, I see!"

Enry grinned. "Wouldn't be without it, Missus."

"Enry!" Bobby ran to his side. "Mam says our Min's going with you!"

Enry bowed. "Always delighted to have the company of a pretty girl – but we best be moving. The lady at the Duck, she's asking for the linen." He lifted the heavy basket with surprising ease, and headed for the door.

Minnie, heavy of heart, followed him.

"Bye, Min!" Bobby blew her a kiss. "Be back soon!"

Once outside, Enry set off at speed, and Minnie was forced to half-run, half-scuttle to keep up. They dodged in and out of the carts and muffin sellers and weary factory girls in order to avoid being pushed over, or having the basket knocked out of Enry's arms.

Despite his over-large boots, the boy was quick on his feet. Minnie couldn't help but admire his agility as he ducked and dived whilst managing to keep the washing safe.

"What's the story, then?" Enry asked as they emerged into a comparatively quiet stretch of road. "Why you keeping me company all of a sudden?" His smile lit up his face as he looked at Minnie. "Weren't for the sake of my handsome hat, and that's for sure."

Minnie couldn't help laughing. She had known Enry for years: he had been coming and going with the washing since he was old enough to stagger under the weight of the basket.

"I tore one of them posh white shirts. Mam says we'll have to pay."

Enry's smile faded. "Marked with an 'O' for *'orrible*, and an 'M' for *misery*?" When Minnie nodded, he shook his head. "That ain't good, Min. They belongs to the Reverend Obadiah Marpike. Tricky piece of work, he is. Never gives me a good word – he's as high and mighty as they come. Most days, he's sour as lemons."

"Oh." Minnie bit her lip. "Well … maybe he'll be having a good day today."

"Maybe," Enry agreed, but he didn't sound hopeful.

They arrived at the back door of the Dog and Duck much too soon for Minnie's liking. Enry winked encouragement at her, put the basket down and tiptoed to a window.

Peering cautiously in, he gave a satisfied nod.

"Looking at a heap of papers," he reported as he came back, "and smoking like a chimney. That's good ... he likes his smokes."

Minnie, cheered by Enry's optimism, followed him into the most enormous kitchen she had ever seen. There were pots and pans hanging from the ceiling, and so many plates, cups and saucers piled up on the shelves of a substantial dresser that she wondered if the Dog and Duck fed the entire population of Middleminster.

The housekeeper, a small woman in a checked apron, caught sight of Enry and came hurrying over. "Enry! Bring that basket over here! I don't want that clean stuff spoiled. Take it up to the laundry room for me, there's a duck." Her eyebrows rose as she noticed Minnie. "And who's this, then? Got yourself a lady friend?"

Enry grinned. "Wouldn't I be the lucky one? This here's a friend of mine: Minnie." He gave Minnie a nudge. "Go on. Tell her!"

Minnie shifted uncomfortably from foot to foot. "It's my mam who does the washing for you, Miss. Marge O'Sullivan. But—" Minnie's legs suddenly felt as if they were about to give way— "I got to tell you, I tore a shirt – one of the good ones. I'm ever so sorry."

"One of the good ones?" The housekeeper stopped laughing. "Was it marked with an 'O' and an 'M'?"

Minnie nodded. "It was the mangle. I got cross, and I pushed too hard."

"Oh, dearie me." The housekeeper sounded worried. "That's not good at all. The Reverend's very particular about his shirts: there's no end of a fuss if there's so much as a shadow of a stain." She paused, and then added, "But he might let you off. We'll see."

She took Minnie by the arm, walking her out of the kitchen and along a low-ceilinged stone-flagged passageway to a heavy oak door. Knocking, she opened it and pulled Minnie inside.

It took Minnie a moment or two to find the tall, thin figure, dressed in clerical black, who was sitting in front of the fire. The room was thick with tobacco smoke – smoke that made her eyes water and her nose run.

It was obviously the man's private sitting room. Books were arranged on a shelf close to his chair, and in front of him was a table heaped with papers, a pen and a large bottle of black ink. It seemed as if he had been hard at work, and had only tidied the papers on hearing the housekeeper's knock on the door; there were ink stains on his hands, and Minnie watched as a glob of black ink slowly trickled from the pen's nib onto the paper beneath.

"Well?" The Reverend Obadiah Marpike's voice was rasping, as if his throat was full of gravel. "What do you want?"

The housekeeper bobbed a curtsy, and pointed at Minnie. "I'm ever so sorry to bother you, Sir, but this young lady has something to confess."

The Reverend Obadiah pulled out a pair of wire-framed glasses, and peered at Minnie. "Confessions, eh? Well, well: confessions are my business. Come here, girl, so I can see you properly."

The housekeeper stepped back politely to wait in the doorway, and Minnie unwillingly did as she was told.

The Reverend's eyes were cold and calculating, and he looked her up and down as if he were assessing her market value. Her heart was beating wildly, but she took a deep breath and did her best to explain.

"If you please, Sir... I got angry – and I knows as I didn't *ought* to get angry, but that old mangle is a beast. I gave the handle an extra turn and I tore one of your shirts, Sir. I'm very sorry indeed, really I am – I wouldn't have done such a thing for all the world—"

Obadiah's expression gave no indication of what he was thinking, and Minnie found herself talking faster and faster, until the reverend gentleman held up his hand to silence her.

As he did so, he knocked the pile of papers off the table and onto the floor and Minnie, hoping to placate him, dived to rescue them.

As she gathered them up, a roughly drawn map caught her eye.

"Oh my!" Her eyes widened; panic made her chatter on. "I knocked all your papers – about mines, are they, Sir?" She glanced again at the page she was holding. "And rubies, too. I never knew they had them kind of mines in other countries... 'Abandoned', it says. Going bust, then, by the looks of it? Who'd have thought—"

There was a sudden eruption from the chair, and Minnie jumped as Obadiah seized her arm in a grip of steel.

"So you can read, can you?" He sneered unpleasantly as he snatched the papers away from her hands. "Did nobody ever tell you it was excessively rude to look at a gentleman's private papers? But of course they didn't. Maggots like you crawl out of the darkest cracks to poison polite society. Your mother lives with a gin bottle constantly at her lips, I have no doubt, and has little inclination to teach her offspring such niceties as manners."

Pictures of her beloved mam swirled in Minnie's mind: Mam heaving herself from the kitchen to the wash house day after day after day; Mam sweating over the steaming copper tub; Mam's sore and swollen hands... And her temper flared.

"Mam never touches the drink! And I'll tell you something, Mister – I'm sorry I tore your shirt, but I'm ever so much sorrier because Mam says she'll have to pay for it, and she don't have nothing, and she'll have to work-work-work – and *that's* what I'm sorriest for!"

Obadiah's face turned purple and, with a muffled oath, he pulled her closer and slapped her hard across the face.

Minnie twisted like an eel, broke his hold and ran … and as she did so, she knocked against the table. The ink bottle tottered, then fell with a crash onto the stone hearth and a pool of black ink spread over the floor and the papers that lay there.

The housekeeper gasped, Obadiah Marpike swore loudly and Minnie hurled herself out of the room, along the passage and into the kitchen.

Panicking, she headed for the door, but the latch stuck, and she began to sob as she tried again and again to open it. At last it lifted, and she tumbled out into the street and went on running.

In and out of the passers-by she flew, gulping for every painful breath, until at last she was at her own door.

Once inside, she flung herself at her mother. "Mam! Mam! I've done a terrible thing and I'm going to be thrown into prison for years and years and years!"

Four

THE REVEREND OBADIAH MARPIKE continued to swear for some considerable time after Minnie's tumultuous exit.

The housekeeper, shaking her head at the violence of his language, went to fetch a dustpan and brush. On her return, however, Obadiah waved her away.

"Do that later," he ordered. "I need to sort my papers!"

As the housekeeper scuttled out, Obadiah threw himself into his chair, and drummed on the table with his fingers.

Curse that little maggot — curse her to the ends of the earth and back again! he thought furiously. *What should I do? She has information that could ruin me ... but does she know it? Of course she doesn't.*

He got to his feet, and began to pace up and down, talking to himself.

"But might she let it slip by mistake? Who does she mix with? A washerwoman's daughter … but a washerwoman who works for the gentry. So there could be danger there: grave danger. Much better if she were put away – but how? A report to the police? Never!"

He gave a mirthless laugh.

"Who knows what discoveries that might lead to? There may yet be those who seek me. I can take no risks; my plans are all but complete. Just one or two more donations to that most noble of causes—" Obadiah paused to sneer— "the Middleminster Literary Ladies Charitable Association for Orphans. And then those donations will be passed on to me, their excellent patron, and all will be done."

Walking to the window, Obadiah stared angrily out as his thoughts whirled. "Let me think, let me think. Children housed in a building with tall walls, and locked doors … could that be the answer?" He glanced down at the broken glass and ink-spoiled papers littering the floor, and his eyes gleamed. "An attack! She attacked me, and an unprovoked attack deserves punishment. Severe punishment! But I … noble and forgiving as I am—" he rolled his eyes, and put his hand over his heart— "I do not wish to give her up to the majesty of the law."

As the idea gradually grew and blossomed in his mind, Obadiah moved back to the table.

"Oh yes. Oh, yes, indeed."

Pulling a clean sheet of paper towards him, he picked up his pen and began to write. Once he had finished his letter, he sanded it, folded it and sealed it with wax. Then, with a grim smile, he picked up the small brass bell that was on the floor beside him, and rang it.

Enry answered the summons; Obadiah nodded at him, and handed him the letter.

"See that this is delivered at once, boy," he said, "and don't waste time!"

Enry gave a half-bow. "Yes, Sir," he replied, and vanished.

Obadiah's smile widened – and it was not a pleasant smile.

"Haddington Hall," he muttered. "That'll stop any of her chatter about my mines … and that most irritating doer of good deeds, Honoria

Haddington, will be overcome with gratitude to the wonderful Reverend Obadiah Marpike for providing her with a suitable inmate!"

After sticking out his tongue at the closed door behind him, Enry ran down the corridor to the kitchen, where he found the housekeeper making a pigeon pie.

"The Reverend wants me to take a note," he said. "That all right with you, Missus?"

The housekeeper slapped a ball of dough onto the marble slab in front of her.

"So he's come to his senses, has he?" She shook her head. "I never heard such language! That friend of yours – she upset him good and proper. Mark you, there were faults on both sides, and I wouldn't say he wasn't just as much to blame as she was."

She slapped the dough a second time.

"All the same, keep her away. Without the Reverend's two guineas a week we'd be in trouble, and that's the gospel truth. So where's this for, then?"

Squinting at the crabbed writing on the note, she read out the address.

"Smart part of town. Garston Street. Make sure you mind your manners, Enry Potter! It's Mrs Haddington you should ask for when you get there."

Enry nodded, and a moment later was running through the streets of Middleminster.

Mrs Haddington's afternoon tea party was going well, or so Mrs Haddington believed. The Middleminster ladies, if asked, might have had reservations: the tea was weak, the sandwiches overly generous on bread and noticeably mean on filling, and the scones so hard that more than one of the visitors gave a sharp squeak, and did her best to conceal the remains in her reticule.

Edith, sitting a little to one side of the group of worthy ladies, had been studying them. She had been introduced as if she herself was one of Mrs Haddington's pet projects, but interest in her had died as soon as the ladies realized she had no exciting tales to tell of the aristocratic high life. And yet again, she decided, her books hadn't painted a true picture: instead of the potential philanthropists demonstrating any interest in the fate of the five children, their conversation was limited to the tricky problem of the removal of stones from greengage jam and other such issues

Mrs Haddington was in her element: now that the drinking of tea from fine bone-china cups was over, she was giving a detailed description of Haddington Hall and the transformational work that was going to take place there.

"Such a delightful place! And bought by generous subscription."

She gave a small self-congratulatory cough.

"We, the Middleminster Literary Ladies' Charitable Association for Orphans, have now achieved what I would describe as a little miracle. Of course—" she coughed again, and a coy expression came over her face— "we owe a great deal to my very dear friend, the Reverend Obadiah Marpike. Such a noble, handsome man. It is he who invests the generous donations that we receive from the good people of Middleminster, and I can assure you, dear ladies, that any offerings you may wish to make will be put to the most excellent use."

Edith, who had already heard quite enough about Mrs Haddington's "very dear friend" Obadiah Marpike, was staring at the ceiling, and wondering about the efficiency of Mrs Haddington's cleaning efforts. The chandelier was thick with dust, several of the crystal drops were missing, and the candles needed replacing.

She was distracted from her thoughts by hearing her name, and looked up in time to hear Mrs Haddington say, "Of course Lady Lavingley is one of our most generous benefactors. She is kind enough to believe in me, as I hope you will too. Even the smallest contribution will be gratefully received."

The ladies nodded and murmured their approval like a flock of elderly Pouter pigeons.

"How wonderful you are, Honoria!"

"An example to us all!"

But there seemed to be a curious hesitation when it came to the opening of purses, and there was more than one suggestion that it must be nearly time to leave their enchanting hostess.

Mrs Haddington's smile was becoming a little fixed when a sour-faced maid appeared with a note on a silver salver. "There's a boy, Ma'am. He brought this. Says he'll wait and see if there's an answer."

Mrs Haddington glanced at the note, and then, recognizing the handwriting, gave a little coo of pleasure.

"Ladies, pray excuse me: a missive from the Reverend Obadiah Marpike. No doubt news of our financial investments…" And she opened the note.

The visitors, always intrigued by the mention of a clergyman, paused in their preparations and were rewarded by a cry of horror. Mrs Haddington clutched at her throat and waved the note dramatically in Edith's direction.

"My dear Edith! Please take this, and read us all this terrible tale that only goes to prove how much children are in need of direction!"

Edith, nothing loath, took the letter. "*My dear Honoria*," she read…

today I was attacked! Viciously attacked in my home – yes, even in the privacy of my own rooms where I live quietly, and at peace with the world. A young girl, the brazen daughter of an infamous washer-woman, burst through the door in order to inform me that she had deliberately destroyed one of my finest lawn shirts. Not only that, but she upset my private papers, and, when asked if she repented of her sins, she declared that her drunken mother was a thousand times more worthy than your humble servant, Obadiah Marpike. She then attacked me as if possessed by the furies, and, when I attempted to defend myself, broke a large bottle of ink over my innocent head.

I have, my dear Honoria, ascertained the name and address of this dangerous young person, and I offer her to you for correction in your most excellent establishment. She appears strong, and with the aid of the strictest rules and the firmest treatment, may yet be of benefit to society, despite a tendency to lie with extraordinary fluency.

Believe nothing she says. Nothing.

My housekeeper has informed me that she can be found in Pocket Yard, Pocket Street. Her name is Minnie O'Sullivan.

P.S. I repeat: **the strictest rules, and the firmest treatment.**

Mrs Haddington swept across the room and took the letter from Edith.

"Our patron has put his faith in me, and I will do as he asks." She gave a dramatic sigh. "It will, of course, take much of my time and energy, but Honoria Haddington knows where her duty lies."

"Oh, Honoria! How wonderful you are!" A little mouse-like woman began to applaud, and her example was quickly followed by the rest of the visitors.

The letter had done what no appeal of Mrs Haddington's own could do, and her dear friends and acquaintances opened their purses with enthusiasm. Those who carried no ready money offered to send notes of promise, and within ten minutes Mrs Haddington's tea party had resulted in an additional income of fourteen guineas.

Edith, impressed by the Literary Ladies' generosity, said, "So I suppose we'll be going to collect Minnie O'Sullivan, Mrs Haddington?"

"Us? Collect a violent and dangerous criminal?" Mrs Haddington looked horrified. "Certainly not! I shall send Ronald, my manservant, early tomorrow morning. You and I, dear Edith, will take ourselves to Haddington Hall and make ready to receive her."

"Should we not go with the manservant?" Edith asked innocently. "Mother never allows me to travel alone, without a female companion."

The ridiculousness of this suggestion made Mrs Haddington close her eyes and reach for her smelling salts – and Edith, realizing that she had overstepped the boundaries of correct and proper manners, said nothing more.

The little mouse-like woman coughed apologetically. "I do think our young friend has made a point. Even if the girl O'Sullivan has no sense of modesty herself, that is no reason to treat her without respect."

Mrs Haddington, still inhaling smelling salts, was thinking hard. She had no desire to be thought of as failing in any way, and, with a self-denying sigh, she said, "Of course. Miss Lavingley and I will collect her ourselves. My manservant will protect us." Turning to the maid, she said, "Kindly inform the boy that the answer is yes … no, wait. I'll write a note."

With a brief apology to her visitors, she went to her bureau and scribbled a brief reply. "Tell the boy to make sure this reaches the Reverend Obadiah Marpike."

"Yes, Ma'am." The maid gave the slightest curtsy, and went to find Enry. He was waiting patiently outside the back door, idly kicking at the boot scraper.

"Got an answer?" he asked.

"Here." The maid handed him the note. "And it's got to be delivered to the Reverend Obadiah Marpike." She sniffed. "Think you can remember that?"

Enry, ignoring the barb in the maid's voice, gave her a wide smile. "I know the Rev." And he was on his way.

He hadn't gone far when a small boy, running like the wind with his head down and two apples clutched in his hands, knocked into Enry and sent him flying. The apples, small boy, Enry and the note landed in a heap; the boy was first up, and grabbing his precious apples was on the run again in seconds.

Enry rubbed his bruised elbows, and picked up the note. As he did so, it fell open and, seeing the name Minnie O'Sullivan, his eyes widened.

Pausing, he had a brief battle with himself, but Minnie's name overruled any hesitation he might have had about reading other people's letters and he began to spell out the words.

My dear Obadiah,

Re: Minnie O'Sullivan

I thank you for putting your trust in me, and I will indeed place this evil and dangerous girl under the strictest supervision at Haddington Hall. Tomorrow will see her safely in my care.

I trust your wounds are mending, and I can only admire your restraint in not immediately throwing her into the hands of the law.

With my most sincere wishes for your recovery,

I am, Dear Sir,

Honoria Haddington

"*Wheeeeee!*" Enry let out a long whistle of astonishment. "What's going on? Min dangerous? Might as well say as that there horse is likely to eat a hippotopamus."

He scratched his head.

"I better keep an eye out for her. The Rev … if he's taken against her, there'll be trouble."

Five

MINNIE HAD SUFFERED A SLEEPLESS NIGHT.
Ever since she had come running home from
the Dog and Duck, she had been waiting for a
policeman to arrive and drag her off to jail –
or, even worse, arrest Mam. It was almost a relief
when there was a hammering on the door early
the following morning.

Mam went to see who it was while Minnie
hovered behind her mother's protective bulk, her
heart battering the walls of her chest. They were
both surprised to see a grim-looking manservant,
who announced with no preamble that his
mistress, Mrs Haddington, would expect Minnie
to be ready for collection later that day.

Mam looked him up and down, and folded
her arms. "Does you mean *my* Minnie?"

"Correct." The manservant stared over Mam's head as if she wasn't worthy of his gaze.

"Well, I wants to know exactly what she's being collected for?"

He pulled a document from his pocket. "All information here. Sign it. If you can, that is." And he slapped the paper on the kitchen table.

Minnie, who had been listening in a disbelieving daze, was shocked into action. She stepped forward and picked up the document.

"Ain't no need to talk to my mam like that!" She gave Roland a disapproving glare. "I been to school: I can write, and I can read, too. Here, Mam..." Giving the paper a quick look, she paled, but there was no wobble in her voice as she said, "Mam – I got to go to a place called Haddington Hall. Sort of a 'norphanage'. I got to learn to be a good girl." Deciding to spare her mother the paragraph describing Minnie as a violent and aggressive young woman, she went on, "You got to put your cross on the line. I'll help you."

"Seems all wrong." Mam rubbed her eyes as Minnie fetched her pen and ink from a shelf. "Signing my daughter away to who knows what."

She looked at Minnie. "You tell me, Min. Did I ought to sign?"

Minnie blinked. Her mother never asked her opinion. Mam O'Sullivan was a woman who knew what was right and what was wrong, and never hesitated to make it clear which was which.

Now, as she looked at her, Minnie's mother seemed to have somehow shrunk inside her huge body, and she wore an expression of agonized indecision that made Minnie's heart ache.

She turned to Roland. "So what happens if it ain't signed?"

Roland shrugged. He had no idea what the answer should be, but he knew his employer would be angry if the document wasn't returned, complete with signature.

"Jail. Or transportation."

A heavy weight settled in Minnie's stomach. "I guess you better sign, Mam."

Mam's hand shook as she made a careful cross. "There." Before the ink had even had time to dry, Roland had snatched it up, and he marched his way out with no word of thanks. As he went, he dusted down his coat in a meaningful fashion before slamming the door behind him.

Minnie and Mam stared at the door, then fell into each other's arms. "Oh, Mam!" Minnie wept, "what will I do without you?"

Mam's eyes were just as wet. "Or me you, Min. You're like my right hand. I never tell you, but you're as good a daughter as anyone could wish for."

Later that morning the mood in Pocket Yard was cheerless. Minnie, dressed in what passed for her best, was sitting at the table. Mam was beside her, and Bobby was holding her hand.

"How long do I have to stay in this place, do you think?" Minnie asked.

Mam shook her head. "How would I know, pet?"

Minnie swallowed. The thought of not knowing whether she would see Mam again for weeks, or months – or even years – was a very terrible one.

Bobby began to cry. "Don't go, Min! I doesn't want you to go!"

"I got no choice," Minnie told him, and she lifted him onto Mam's knee. "I'll write to you. I'll send letters to Aunt Bet, and she can read them to you … and I'll tell you when I'm coming back, just as soon as I knows."

As if on cue, there came the sound of heavy footsteps outside, followed by a sharp knock on the door. Minnie went white, and Bobby began to cry louder. Mam, her face set and pale, put Bobby down and engulfed Minnie in a hug so fierce that Minnie gasped.

"Be good, now, my Min. Work hard."

She let Minnie go as suddenly as she had hugged her, and turned away with a muffled sob.

The sight of her mother's heaving shoulders made Minnie brave. "I'll get the door," she said. "Don't cry." And she blinked away her own tears. "Look after yourself, Mam. Dearest Mam."

She stopped, and shut her eyes in an effort to stop herself from rushing to hide herself for ever in her mother's comforting arms.

"I won't make a fuss, and I'll work ever so hard, you see if I don't … and I'll be back afore you knows it. Bobs, you be careful with that mangle! It's your job now."

And then, with her head held high, Minnie went to open the door. Roland was waiting outside, a substantial cudgel in his hand in case of opposition. Minnie, wide-eyed and clutching a ragged bundle of possessions, bobbed a curtsy.

"I'm ready, if you please."

"Get walking," Roland growled. "Carriage is at the end of the street. Try and run, and I'll have you before you've got a yard."

Minnie tossed her head. "Never even thought of it! Said as I was ready, didn't I?"

And she walked steadily to where the carriage was waiting.

Six

As Minnie reached the carriage door, Mrs Haddington pulled her skirts away as if the girl was infectious.

Edith, sitting on the other side of the carriage, noticed, and she leant forward to greet Minnie with a smile. "How do you do?" she said. "I saw you carrying a bucket of coal, I think?"

Mrs Haddington, horrified at Edith's warmth, tut-tutted loudly before Minnie could answer.

"Get in, girl! I am your benefactor, Mrs Haddington, and Miss Lavingley is my companion." She looked Minnie up and down with a sneer. "I shall call you Mangle. I understand your mother is a washerwoman—" her tone suggested that this was an occupation she found offensive in the extreme— "so it will be appropriate."

Minnie bit her lip, but didn't answer. As she climbed into the carriage, her little bundle fell, and she gave a cry of distress.

"Leave it, Mangle!" Mrs Haddington ordered. "You will be provided with clothes at Haddington Hall. You will also be thoroughly washed and checked for lice."

Minnie flushed. "I ain't lousy, Missus. My mam's a washerwoman, and she keeps us neat as pins. And that's my undies in there, and my pen and ink from my old teacher, and I needs them for writing letters."

Edith was feeling deeply uncomfortable. Not knowing how else to show her dislike of Mrs Haddington's attitude, she slipped out of the carriage and collected Minnie's bundle.

"Here," she said as she placed it on the girl's lap. "Keep it safe!"

"Ta ever so, Miss!" Minnie's face lit up in a smile. Then her smile faded, and she gave Mrs Haddington a cold look. "Mam made sure as I had nothing but clean stuff. Clean from top to toe, I am."

Mrs Haddington's face darkened. She was remembering the Reverend Obadiah Marpike's letter, and his instructions that this girl was to be treated with the utmost severity.

"You will speak only when you are spoken to!" she snapped. "I expect you to be silent at all other times. It will give you time to reflect upon your wicked and evil behaviour yesterday … your unprovoked attack upon a defenceless and innocent man of the church."

Minnie's temper flared. "What evil behaviour? I busted the bottle of ink when I knocked into the gentleman's table, but it weren't on purpose. It was bad, I knows that, and that's why I'm here. And I'm sorry as I tore his shirt. But Mam says as evilness is when you means to be bad, like when you does a murder, or when you hurts someone if they never did you no harm, or—"

"Enough!" Mrs Haddington had never expected a lecture on morality from a girl who lived in Pocket Yard. "I know the truth of the matter, and your lies mean nothing to me. Not another word, or you will be beaten severely upon arrival at Haddington Hall."

"I never tell lies," Minnie began, but Edith put her hand over Minnie's and squeezed it.

"*Shhh,*" she whispered as the carriage rattled loudly over the cobbles. "Best not to argue."

Unwillingly, Minnie did as she was told, but the injustice of Mrs Haddington's remarks continued to burn inside her.

Nobody noticed the tall lad who slid out from between two houses as the heavy carriage went rumbling away, and nobody noticed him as he followed close behind.

Street after street they travelled, until they were on the other side of the city, but Enry never faltered in his steady pursuit.

Got to see where she's going, he told himself. *Haddington Hall: never heard of it. And what's going to happen to our Min when she gets there?* He shook his head. *Sounds like they got it in for her... So this place will be no picnic.*

Minnie, too, was wondering what Haddington Hall would be like. Having been sworn to silence, she couldn't ask any of the questions that were bubbling in her mind.

She gave Edith a sideways look, but all she received in return was a smile.

But Edith also had questions. She had been shocked by the way Mrs Haddington had treated Minnie, and the manner in which she had spoken to her.

It was cruel, she told herself. *And she claims to be a philanthropist! It almost sounded as if she was enjoying herself...* She shivered. *And Mrs Haddington's friend. He says he was attacked – but Minnie says all she did was break a bottle of ink. I don't understand.*

Mrs Haddington, meanwhile, was entirely unaware of Edith's feelings. She assumed her friendly overtures towards Minnie were due to the two girls being similar in age, and considered her behaviour to be the result of inexperience and a sheltered upbringing.

Leaning back against the cushions, Mrs Haddington congratulated herself on an excellent morning's work. *By the end of today we will have three girls in residence! And two more to follow shortly,* she thought – and allowed herself a charming fantasy of being praised for her charitable achievements by none other than the queen herself. *I will, perhaps, be presented at court. An invitation will be sent, and I shall respond most graciously.* The fantasy grew, and blossomed. *We might go together, Obadiah and I. Such a very charming man! A man who truly appreciates the aims and ambitions of my little charity. And a man—* Mrs Haddington, a widow of many years' standing, actually began to blush at her next thought— *a man who appreciates me!*

By the time the carriage drew up outside the orphanage, it had begun to rain: a steady downpour that showed no sign of stopping.

Mrs Haddington insisted on sheltering Edith under her umbrella – a difficult business, as both had substantial skirts and the path was narrow.

Minnie was ordered to walk in front of them, with Roland in attendance in case she made a last attempt to dash for freedom. By the time they reached the front door, Minnie's thin dress was soaked through, and her flame-red hair was dripping in rats' tails.

Pride kept her back straight and her tears at bay, but her first sight of the house had made icy-cold fingers squeeze her heart.

It looks like it's rotting away, she thought. *Makes home look like a blooming palace.*

The creaking front door proved difficult to open. Mrs Krick could be heard muttering as she tugged from the other side, and it took a hefty shove from the muscular Roland before the door finally gave up.

"Hurry up, girl! Don't keep us waiting in the rain!" Mrs Haddington sounded as if she thought the bad weather was all Minnie's fault.

Mrs Krick stepped to one side, and Minnie walked into Haddington Hall to be greeted by her dog Gobbler, hackles up and growling.

"Oh my sainted Lord Jesus, Mary and the angels!" Minnie gasped, and froze as Gobbler circled round her, sniffing at her ankles.

Mrs Haddington gave a sharp cry of horror, and Minnie looked at her, expecting her to call the dog off – but it was Minnie's exclamation that had shocked her, not the dog's behaviour.

"Minnie O'Sullivan! Did I hear you take the Lord's name in vain? You'll wash your mouth out with soap right now this minute! Take her upstairs, Mrs Krick, and see to it at once!"

Mrs Krick looked sullen.

"That's not for me to do." She pointed at Edith. "Let her do it, seeing as she's meant to be helping."

"Oh!" Edith saw the possibility of being able to talk to Minnie on her own. "Of course I will."

This was not at all what Mrs Haddington wanted, but neither did she want a confrontation with the housekeeper. Mrs Krick was a bargain; it would be exceedingly difficult to replace her for the same paltry wages.

She frowned, before unwillingly agreeing. "You can use the opportunity to wash your hands, Edith. With carbolic soap! And wash them again if you touch the girl."

"Of course, Mrs Haddington. Thank you." Edith was trying hard to sound obedient, but there was an unusual gleam in her eyes as she and Minnie walked up the narrow stairs.

Reaching the top, Edith tried a door, but it seemed to be locked; it was only when an angry voice from inside told her to "Go away! We ain't coming out!" that she realized it was being held shut from the other side.

Minnie, meanwhile, had opened another door, and found a long dormitory room.

Five iron beds were arranged down one wall; two had evidently been slept in, as they had thin grey blankets piled on the tops. The other beds had nothing but bare straw mattresses, and she shivered at the thought of trying to keep warm at night.

Ain't going to get much shut-eye there, she thought. *Freezing now … it'll be like an ice house come night-time.*

At the far end was a washstand, with a ewer of cold water and a large dish of soap. Minnie moved as if to go towards it, but Edith sat down on the edge of one of the beds.

"Please," she said, "can you tell me why you're here?" Seeing Minnie's look of surprise, she added, "I do want to know… Just as long as you don't mind telling me, of course. I know that there was a reverend gentleman involved: I read the letter he sent to Mrs Haddington, claiming that you attacked him."

Minnie hesitated. Was this some kind of trap?

"I never did no such thing, Miss."

"What exactly happened?"

Edith's expression was sympathetic, and indignation at the lies that had been told got the better of Minnie. "He called my mam names, Miss. I wasn't going to stand for that, was I? So I told him how my mam works harder than anybody! And I was boiling mad – but I never touched him. He slapped me, and I upset the table when I ran away." Honesty made her add, "I did break his ink bottle. The mess was something shocking, all over his precious papers, but I didn't mean harm."

Edith's eyes widened. "I'd have tipped the bottle of ink over his head," she said. "No wonder you ran away. But why didn't you tell your mother? Or the servants? Surely they'd have defended you against him?"

"Mam's got a temper," said Minnie, "and she'd have gone mad and tried to kill him. The housekeeper ... well, the Reverend pays her money, don't he? She ain't going to kill the goose that lays the golden eggs."

Edith blinked. "But that's not fair!"

"Mam says there's one law for the rich, and another for the poor, and there ain't no skipping between them."

Minnie had heard this so often she could hardly believe Edith didn't know it as well. It was ingrained into her very bones, and was the rule by which Mam lived her life.

There was a long, thoughtful pause before Edith spoke again, and when she did, she sounded humble.

"I have a lot to learn about things, Minnie. All I know is from reading books ... and they don't seem to tell the truth." A noise from downstairs made her jump to her feet. "Oh: I almost forgot. We've got to pretend you've had your mouth washed out! What shall we do?"

"Wash our hands, Miss." Minnie went over to the washstand, and inspected the soap with a professional eye.

"That's rubbish, that is. No good for washing nothing, soap like this." She banged the bar against the table, and a chunk fell off. "Look at that! But it smells ever so strong. Her, downstairs – she'll never know we didn't do it."

Mrs Haddington heard their laughter, and made a mental resolution to keep the two girls apart in future.

Laughter was not something she intended to encourage.

Peg and Molly had also heard, and as Edith and Minnie came out of the dormitory, the door of the linen room was opened and Peg peered out.

"What's the joke?" she demanded, and then, seeing Edith's clothes, she added, "Here, Molly! Come and look at this... We got a real posh dresser, and no mistake."

Leaning out of the doorway, she snatched at Edith's shawl.

"Give us that!"

"Give it back." Minnie caught the edge of the shawl, and glared at Peg. "Leave Miss alone! She's – she's..." Minnie was struggling to think of the right way to describe Edith. "She's nice!"

"Don't care how she is." Peg gave the shawl a sharp tug. "Give it here!"

Minnie's temper rose, and her eyes flashed as she gave the shawl such a forceful yank that Peg staggered, and let go.

"I'm here to help Mrs Haddington." Edith, taken aback by Peg's sudden attack, sounded prim. "Thank you, Minnie..."

"*Thenk yew*, Minnie!" Peg mimicked. "Ooooh! You got a posh friend, have you, Minnie? Well, just you wait till she ain't around. I'll pay you back good and proper! And you, Miss Goody Two Shoes—" she gave Edith a venomous glare— "you tell that old cow downstairs that if she don't shut that dog away, me and Moll are going to get ourselves out of here, and there ain't nothing as she can do about it."

And she went back into the linen room, slamming the door behind her.

"Oh dear," Edith said. "I'm so sorry, they... They don't seem very friendly. Will you be all right?"

Minnie shrugged. "Guess so." She gave Edith a rueful smile. "But that girl made the dog look like a pal!"

Seven

ENRY, PUFFING HARD, HAD ARRIVED AT Haddington Hall too late to see who had got out of Mrs Haddington's carriage. Keeping under the shadows of the dripping trees, and out of the view of Roland and the coachman, he inspected the building with interest.

So that's where Minnie's going to be, he thought. *Bet the mould would grow in between your toes if you stayed too long. Skellingtons in the attics, and rats in the cellars – but I reckon even they wouldn't hang about here.*

Deciding he was so wet that more rain couldn't possibly hurt him, he made up his mind to walk round the cottage and see what happened at the back. There he found an abandoned vegetable garden, knee-high in thistles and weeds.

It was overlooked by a long row of windows tucked under the roof, and another couple at ground level that belonged to Mrs Krick's sitting room and kitchen.

There was a broken-down fence that had been roughly mended with wire and string; it wasn't difficult to climb over, and when Enry saw a dilapidated shed on the other side, the thought came to him that he could find shelter there.

His stomach rumbled loudly as he crept towards his hiding place, and reminded him that he hadn't eaten anything that day; a quick look round showed him the remains of a row of turnips, and his eyes shone.

With a grunt of satisfaction, Enry pulled up the largest and, brushing the earth off it, glanced over his shoulder to make sure he was unobserved. There was no sign of life from the orphanage, and a moment later he was settled in the shed and chewing hard.

The turnip was old, and Enry was forced to abandon most of it. He had done his best, but it would have taken weeks of boiling to make it edible. Sighing, he lobbed the remains into a corner. It then occurred to him that where there were turnips, there might also be carrots or onions. The rain had eased a little, and he took a couple of steps towards Haddington Hall.

A line of washing was swaying in the wind, and he looked at the striped yellow-and-black dresses with interest.

Just like a row of dancing wopsies, he thought.

Squinting upwards, he was rewarded by a glimpse of Minnie and Edith at one of the up-stairs windows.

There's our Min... But who's that with her? Seems like they're getting on, friendly like — and that's good. He smiled to himself. *Wonder if she's seen Min in one of her tempers? Makes the sparks fly, and no mistake, but then it's all blue skies and, "Sorry, Enry, have a cup of tea".*

Hoping to get a clearer look, he pushed through the thistles ... and was met with a flurry of barking.

The kitchen door opened and Gobbler burst out, ears flattened and teeth bared.

Enry gasped, and fled. As he hurled himself over the fence, his hat fell off, and he was forced to leave it lying amongst the turnips.

Mrs Krick, watching from the kitchen window, rubbed her hands together.

"That'll teach him a lesson, and no mistake."

She went to report Gobbler's success to Mrs Haddington, but the philanthropist was concerned to hear that there had been an intruder.

"Did he look dangerous?" she asked.

"Nothing as Gobbler can't deal with," Mrs Krick said. "Saw him off in two ticks."

This was what Mrs Haddington wanted to hear. She nodded, and gave Mrs Krick a patronizing smile. "Good. A fine dog."

The fine dog began to growl, and Mrs Haddington saw Minnie had come downstairs with Edith. She noticed with pleasure that Minnie was smelling strongly of cheap carbolic; reassured that her instructions had been carried out, she demanded, "You! Why aren't you wearing your uniform?"

Minnie looked blank. "Uniform, Miss? I don't got no uniform."

"Really? Are you blind as well as stupid? There's a dress laid out on every bed!"

Edith intervened. "I'm sorry, Mrs Haddington, but we didn't see any dresses up there."

"What?" Mrs Haddington gave Mrs Krick a suspicious look. "Did you not do as I asked? Where are the uniforms?"

"On the line."

Mrs Krick pointed to the kitchen door, and folded her arms.

"Needed airing, so I hung 'em out. Over and above what I'm paid for, too: it's not for me to look after the girls. That's Nellie, whenever she condescends to get here – that's her job."

Mrs Haddington tutted in irritation, but gave in. "Very well. Mangle – bring the dresses in, and take them upstairs."

"I'll help her," Edith said quickly.

"There'll be no need for that, thank you, Miss Lavingley." Mrs Haddington's reply was frosty. "Mangle can manage perfectly well on her own." Seeing Mrs Krick look puzzled, she explained, "Her mother is a washerwoman. While she is here, she will be known as Mangle."

Minnie stood up very straight. "There ain't nothing wrong with being a washerwoman! And, if you please, I'd rather be called Minnie."

"If I say you're to be called Mangle, then that's what you'll answer to." Mrs Haddington pressed her thin lips together, and her eyes narrowed. "Now, go with Mrs Krick and collect the dresses, take them upstairs, and lay one on each bed. Change into yours, then come back down, bringing your old clothes with you. They will be burned."

Minnie went scarlet with anger, but a growl from Gobbler made her pause just long enough to notice Edith shaking her head. Understanding that this was a warning, she made a heroic effort to suppress her feelings.

"Yes, Miss."

"Don't call me 'Miss'!" Mrs Haddington snapped. "You are to call me 'Madam'."

"Yes, Madam."

"And curtsy when you answer me. You're nothing, Mangle – do you know that? Nothing."

Edith, watching, felt a wave of nausea. *She's a monster*, she thought. *She's not just nasty… She's a complete and utter bully!*

As Minnie staggered up the stairs carrying the dresses, Edith's head continued to whirl. If she walked out of Haddington Hall, as she would very much like to do, where would that leave Minnie?

Her thoughts were interrupted when Minnie reappeared, dressed in the hideous black and yellow dress, which was far too big for her; a white linen apron was tied twice round her waist and that, too, trailed on the floor.

Minnie seemed to have shrunk, and her expression was forlorn. A small bundle was under her arm, and Mrs Haddington immediately pounced on it.

"Take these disgusting garments into the kitchen and burn them, and make sure you wash your hands afterwards. Mangle will help you in the kitchen, Mrs Krick – make sure she's kept busy at all times."

"But Minnie will surely share in the lessons with the others?" Edith asked as Minnie followed Mrs Krick down the dark passage that led to the kitchen.

Mrs Haddington shook her head. "The Reverend Obadiah Marpike specifically asked me to remember that Mangle has a history of violence. It would not be appropriate to allow her to join the other girls at their lessons."

She sniffed, as if the very mention of Minnie reminded her of something unpleasant.

"She will have to sleep in the dormitory at night, since there is no other provision for her, but she will rise before the other girls in order to clean the kitchen and prepare breakfast."

Edith opened her mouth to say she disagreed, then closed it again. She needed time to think – but then a sharp knock on the front door made them both turn.

Mrs Krick came shuffling out from the kitchen, and the door was, with much effort, opened to reveal the sour-faced parlour maid who had served tea in Mrs Haddington's house.

She was carrying a leather bag, and looked even more sullen than she had the previous day. As she glanced into the gloomy hallway, her face darkened further, but she made no comment.

"Ah, Nellie!" Mrs Haddington greeted her with a brief nod. "You're here at last."

Nellie glowered at her. "I came as soon as I could, Ma'am … but the omnibus, it don't go near here. I had to walk."

"No matter!" Mrs Haddington dismissed the complaint with an imperious wave of her hand. "Mrs Krick, this is Nellie Addams, my parlour maid."

The housekeeper and the parlour maid looked at each other with equal suspicion, as meanness recognized spitefulness.

"Pleased to meet you, I'm sure," said Nellie, and Mrs Krick nodded.

"How do you do?" she replied. "About time you were here, if you don't mind my saying so." She sniffed. "Housekeeper, that's what I was employed for — the girls are all yours. There's three of them now, and two more due."

Mrs Haddington was satisfied, but Edith was overcome with doubts. Was this really the young woman that Mrs Haddington had described as doting on children? A second mother?

But the philanthropist was already sweeping her out of the door.

"Come along, Edith. We'll leave Nellie to settle in."

"But we'll be coming back?" Edith asked, then wondered if she had sounded too eager. Crossing her fingers while she told the lie, she added, "I know my mother will be eager to hear how the girls progress. Lady Lavingley—" she crossed her fingers more tightly still— "is so very interested in your work."

"In that case," Mrs Haddington said with a delighted smile, "we shall return as soon as the orphan sisters arrive. Roland is to collect them this afternoon, or perhaps tomorrow."

She considered the matter for a moment.

"Let us say that we will return here tomorrow morning."

And with that, Edith had to be content.

Eight

MINNIE HEARD THE RUMBLE OF WHEELS as the carriage rolled away. She had been sent into the garden to look for vegetables, but a wave of homesickness had engulfed her and she had allowed herself to cry.

Now, holding a bunch of elderly carrots and a couple of cabbages that had been enjoyed by a host of caterpillars, she opened the kitchen door and went in. Gobbler, lying on an old blanket, greeted her with a low growl, but didn't bother to get to his feet.

"And what do you call those?" Mrs Krick gave the carrots a despising glance.

"It's all weeds out there," Minnie said. "The veggies are smothered." She rubbed her hand on her apron. "Stingers, too."

"Should have been more careful." Mrs Krick was not sympathetic. "This afternoon you get out there and clear that garden, stingers or no stingers. Now, I want those cleaned!"

Minnie did as she was told. As she scrubbed at the carrots, she was still thinking about Mam and Bobby, and a tear trickled down her cheek.

"Oi." Mrs Krick had noticed. "Cut that out. Feeling sorry for yourself? From what Mrs H says, you're lucky you didn't get thrown in jail."

Nellie had come into the kitchen while Mrs Krick was speaking, and she raised her eyebrows.

"What's that? You got a jailbird skivvying in here, have you?" Her eyes swept scornfully over Minnie.

Minnie swung round from the sink, and glared at Nellie. "I ain't no jailbird! I lives with my mam."

"Got a temper, I see." There was calculation in Nellie's cold eyes. "Been sent here for stealing?"

Minnie's grip tightened on her scrubbing brush. "I ain't never stole nothing! Mam brought me and Bobby up straight and true. She'd have the hide off us if we nicked so much as a farthing!"

Mrs Krick looked disbelieving. "Easy enough for you to say." She turned to Nellie. "I'll show you the upstairs, seeing as you're in charge of the girls. You – Mangle – put on the kettle."

And she led Nellie out of the kitchen, leaving Minnie alone.

With a sigh, Minnie finished the carrots and began to clean the cabbage.

"Euch!" A large green caterpillar wiggled at her, and she took a step back.

At once Gobbler raised his head, and growled faintly.

"Ain't no use you growling at me," Minnie told him. "Won't make me work any faster. Don't suppose you eat caterpillars, do you?"

Gobbler's ears twitched, and the growling stopped.

Minnie, encouraged by even this tiny sign of friendship, went on, "Been living here long? Not much of a place, is it?"

She opened the window and dropped the caterpillar out into the garden, then returned to her cabbage. Once that was done, she boiled the kettle, but was unable to find any tea despite searching various tins and boxes.

Discovering an old and mouldy crust, she threw it to Gobbler, who ate it with such enthusiasm that Minnie inspected him more closely than she had before.

"Gor! Nothing but skin and bone, are you? No wonder you wants to eat us all. Bet you never gets a square meal from that old witch ... and don't suppose I will, neither."

A very faint wag of Gobbler's tail suggested that he agreed with her, and Minnie, greatly daring, put out a hand to pat him.

At once he growled, and she hurriedly drew back from him.

"I said to you," she told the dog. "No point growling. Now, I better ask about that tea."

Taking a deep breath, she went to find the housekeeper. She discovered Mrs Krick sitting with Nellie in her sitting room, a cosy little room with a roaring fire and two comfortable armchairs. A table was neatly laid with flowered china teacups, with a large teapot as the centrepiece.

On being asked where Minnie could find the tea, Mrs Krick unlocked a box on the mantelpiece, and carefully measured out the necessary tea leaves.

"Make sure the water's boiling, and don't you go dropping that teapot! That was a present and if you break it, there'll be trouble like you've never seen."

Nellie gave a spiteful chuckle as Minnie left the room.

"You'll not be getting any teapots from our Mrs H, I'd say. Mean as a weasel, that one."

"Is that so?" Mrs Krick was eager to hear gossip about her employer.

"Pays me nothing." Nellie was only concerned with her own grievances. "Orders me over here, and expects me to teach them girls cleaning and sewing, and not a penny more does she offer!"

She leant forward.

"And let's get something straight. I ain't intending to work my fingers to the bone. Done more than enough of that, thank you very much."

Mrs Krick gave her a sideways look. "Getting you to teach the girls, is she? What for? All part of her good works, is it?"

Nellie gave a derisive laugh. "Good works? Ain't nothing but interfering in other folks' business."

The scorn in her voice would have shocked Mrs Haddington to the core.

"Got more money than sense, she has. That's what them rich folks do. Think they can play at being God – but it's interfering, like I says." She sniggered. "You should have heard them talking at her last tea party. 'Oh, Mrs Dogooder ... how wonderful you are. Devoting your life to charitable causes! I only hope as I can do my own little part to help the poor and afflicted like as what you have.' And then they pays out money in silver shillings and golden sovereigns, while we earns pennies and halfpennies. Makes me sick."

Nellie's imitation of a Middleminster lady was remarkably accurate, but Minnie had reappeared with the teapot, and Mrs Krick hastily changed the subject.

"Mangle! There's a pile of pots and pans in the scullery – go and wash them clean." To Nellie, she said, "I got to warn you. Mangle's got a vicious temper. That's why she's in the kitchen, not with the others."

Nellie looked knowing. "I could tell, soon as I saw her. Not been brought up proper."

Minnie, pausing in the doorway, was unable to stop herself from a sharp reply. "I was brought up properer than you! My mam, she always said it was rude to talk to folks the way you talks to me."

A satisfied smile crossed Nellie's sour little face. "Just like you says, Mrs Krick. Temper!"

Mrs Krick nodded. "See how she answers back? Flares up quicker than oil on flames. That temper needs breaking, Mrs H says."

Minnie left the room, making sure that she slammed the door behind her, and the gleam in Nellie's eyes grew brighter.

Back in the small, spider-infested scullery that was next to the kitchen, Minnie faced a pile of dirty pots and pans.

Her confrontation with Nellie had unnerved her; she knew all too well that she had made an enemy. *But no one's slagging off my mam*, she told herself, and she began to scrub a particularly unpleasant porridge pan as fiercely as if it were Nellie herself.

Thoughts of the future kept floating through her mind, and she scrubbed harder in order to suppress a rising sense of panic.

A low growl interrupted her thoughts again, and she looked down to see Gobbler standing close beside her, his eyes fixed greedily on the dirty saucepans and plates.

"Most of it's burnt," Minnie warned him. "You must be ever so hungry to fancy any of that."

By way of an experiment, she put a filthy old stew pan on the floor; Gobbler leapt at it with such ferocity that Minnie gasped.

"Love a duck. When did you last eat?"

Several saucepans later, Gobbler seemed to have had enough. Licking his chops, he left the scullery to go back to his bed on the kitchen floor, but not before giving Minnie a grateful wag of his tail.

She looked after him as he went, shaking her head. "No wonder he were wanting to bite everybody! Ain't been fed for weeks, I'd say. Well … if burnt pans is going to keep him happy, that's easy enough."

With a sigh she turned back to her washing-up. Gobbler had done a good job, but every pan still needed scrubbing, and the pile diminished gradually.

When there were only a few pots left, Minnie paused for a moment, and wiped the small, grubby pantry window so she could see out to the garden beyond. The rain had changed to a light drizzle, and the leaves of the overgrown cabbage plants gleamed faintly as the sun tried to break through the heavy clouds.

Something caught her eye, and she squinted to see what it was.

A bag? A hat? It had the look of a hat … or was it something else?

"Ouch!"

Mrs Krick had slapped at Minnie's wrist with a dirty tea cloth. "I'll have no wishy-washy daydreaming from you, my girl! You're here to work, not stare out of windows!" And she stormed away.

I'll have a look later, Minnie told herself … but there was no opportunity. Mrs Krick kept her hard at work until it was late evening, and Minnie was exhausted.

All she had eaten since leaving home were peelings from the carrots, and a scoop of the evening meal's leftover cabbage soup. The soup had been rejected by Peg and Molly as unfit for human consumption, and Minnie had hoped she would be allowed at least a bowlful.

But Nellie, with a gleeful grin, had poured it away in front of Minnie's hungry eyes.

"That'll teach you to answer me back, jailbird!"

Minnie, too tired and weary to react, took the pan and went to wash it clean.

Now it was nearly midnight.

Peg and Molly, who still hadn't set foot downstairs apart from a brief dash to collect their food, had claimed all the blankets by the time Minnie was finally allowed to make her way to the dormitory.

Her narrow bed with its straw-filled mattress was cold and uninviting and, when she sat down, sharp stalks poked through the cheap cotton cover and scratched her.

Seeing that Peg was awake, she crept over to her.

"Give us just one blanket," she begged.

Peg peered at Minnie from under a couple of the sought-after blankets.

"Go find your posh friend. We ain't talking to you."

And she pulled the coverings over her head.

Minnie, aching in every limb, went slowly back to her own bed.

Taking off her enormous apron, she laid it over the mattress, and tried to pretend she was warm and comfortable ... but it was impossible.

Molly had begun to snore loudly, and Peg was whistling through her nose; Minnie, chilled to the bone and completely miserable, lay with her eyes open, wondering what would become of her.

Even that dog has a blanket, she thought, and with the thought came an idea.

As silently as she could, Minnie crept out of bed and across the dormitory floor. At the top of the stairs, she stopped to listen – she had no idea where Mrs Krick and Nellie had their bed-rooms, but presumed they were near Mrs Krick's sitting room.

Hearing nothing except for Molly's steady snoring, she tiptoed down the stairs: even the thought of waking Gobbler paled beside the thought of the warm kitchen.

As silently as a ghost, she glided down the dark corridor and, as she had expected, the door was open so that Gobbler could, should he so wish, roam the house.

"Oh!" It took Minnie an enormous effort not to scream. Something warm and living was pressing against her long skirt; putting out a tentative hand, she realized it was the dog.

"Hello," she whispered, and then, "Ta ever so for not barking."

Tentatively, she scratched the top of his head. He responded by leaning against her, evidently enjoying the unaccustomed petting.

"Good boy," Minnie told him, and she tiptoed further into the kitchen. The kitchen range had been banked up for the night, but it was still warm … much warmer than the cold and clammy dormitory upstairs.

Even though the room was dark, Minnie was able to find Gobbler's blanket. She wrapped it round her, and despite its many holes and tears felt a comforting warmth.

A moment later Gobbler came to join her. He appeared quite happy to share his bed, and settled down with a grunt and a wag of his tail. Minnie even put her arm round him, and was surprised to feel him wriggle with pleasure.

Before long the two of them were curled up together and fast asleep.

Nine

IT WAS BARELY LIGHT WHEN GOBBLER woke Minnie by licking her face. She sat up with a start, wondering where on Earth she was; when she remembered, she was unable to stop herself from sighing.

The dog was looking at her hopefully, and she realized he wanted to be fed. Sadly she shook her head at him.

"Ain't nothing for neither of us," she said. "And I better get my pinny."

Jumping to her feet, she crept out of the kitchen and back to the dormitory to collect her apron. Peg and Molly were both still sound asleep, and never stirred as she washed her face and hands in the ice-cold water in the ewer, and brushed the dust off her dress.

Tying the apron round her waist, she went downstairs and was just in time to meet Mrs Krick emerging bleary-eyed from her own quarters.

"Up already? You better not be thieving, or I'll set Gobbler on you. Get that range sorted, and be quick about it."

As she spoke Mrs Krick kicked the dog, who growled fiercely.

The range was old, and very like the range Minnie was used to. The coals were still too hot to touch with her bare hands; finding an old iron shovel, she began the laborious job of cleaning it, laying fresh wood and coal, and lighting it from the glowing embers left over from the night before.

When it was finally done, she pulled herself to her feet.

Mrs Krick had left a cracked mug of watery milk on the table, together with a couple of broken crusts; this, Minnie assumed, was her breakfast.

She could easily have eaten twice as much, but she shared half and half with her new friend. Despite her enormous weariness, she was intrigued to see Gobbler's attitude change the moment Mrs Krick came back into the kitchen.

Instead of sitting at Minnie's feet and gazing adoringly at her, he stood four-square with his head lowered, and growled deep in his chest as the housekeeper put on the kettle and unlocked one of the cupboards.

Taking out a loaf of fresh bread, and seeing Minnie's expression, she indicated the door with her head.

"Get out. This here's for me and Nellie. Make yourself useful, and get on with clearing that garden."

Minnie did as she was told. The air outside was cool, and the long grass and weeds brushed damply against her skirts, but it was a relief to be out of the house and she looked eagerly about her.

What was it she had seen the day before? Slowly, so as not to draw attention to what she was doing, she moved towards the end of the garden, pulling up handfuls of thistles and weeds as she went. From time to time, she unearthed an onion or a carrot; these, she tied in the corner of her shawl, thinking they might come in useful.

Then she found it: a top hat.

It was old, and worn well beyond the time when most hats were thrown away, but it was clear that it hadn't been in the garden long – when she turned it over, it was dry inside.

Staring at it, Minnie knew who the owner was. How many times had she seen Enry Potter come whistling into her kitchen, wearing that very hat? Just the sight of it reminded her of home, and of Enry's cheerful smile.

Minnie looked round, but there was no sign of anyone. The dilapidated garden shed was only a couple of yards away; could Enry possibly be hiding there?

A quick glance over her shoulder reassured her that no one was watching from the windows of Haddington Hall. Creeping to the open door, Minnie looked inside. The shed was empty, as she had more than half expected – but the half-chewed turnip spoke volumes.

"Enry's been here, for sure," she told herself. "And he must have been looking for me. Why else would he have come to a horrible place like this?"

The thought of Enry searching for her was comforting and, hanging the hat on a rusty nail, she sat down beside an old wooden bucket to consider the idea.

"Ain't no sign of him now … but might he come back again?"

The thought of rescue was almost too much to bear, and she wiped her eyes on the edge of her shawl. An onion slipped into the bucket, and she tipped the rest of the vegetables after it before preparing to return to her weeding.

As she stepped back into the garden, she was met by a loud screech of "Mangle? *Mangle? MANGLE!*"

Mrs Krick was standing at the kitchen door, her face like thunder. As Minnie came towards her, she began to mutter darkly, and Minnie's heart fluttered. Thinking fast, she held out the bucket: "I got a pail of veggies. There's more if you want."

Certain that Minnie had been trying to escape, the housekeeper was taken aback by this offering.

"Weren't no need for you to go up the end," was all she could think of by way of reply.

Minnie nodded. "Yes, Mrs Krick. But most of the veggies are up the end… There's a whole row of turnips. Did you want me to go on clearing them thistles?"

The housekeeper shook her head. "You're needed in here to wash the kitchen floor. Mrs H will be here any minute."

With a last glance at the garden, Minnie did as she was told. As she came into the kitchen, Gobbler greeted her with a thump of his tail, and she was cheered.

At least the dog likes me, she thought, and she went to fetch the mop and pail.

Mrs Haddington was indeed on her way to Haddington Hall, together with Edith.

The philanthropist was glowing; the Reverend Obadiah Marpike had done her the honour of paying a call earlier that morning, and had praised her fundraising abilities to the skies.

"Fourteen guineas, my dear Honoria! It shall be invested in the safest of my projects, and I promise that you will see the most remarkable return on your money."

He waved a newspaper in front of his hostess's nose, a little too quickly for her to read.

"As I'm sure a fashionable woman such as yourself will be aware, rubies are in the highest demand just now. Investment in the

Seventy-Seventh Mogok mine will bring you a small fortune."

He bowed low, and his smile imitated that of the stuffed crocodile that graced Mrs Haddington's withdrawing room.

"I look forward to seeing a necklace of the finest rubies in your possession. Rubies should only be worn by ladies of distinction and charm, such as yourself."

Mrs Haddington waved her hand in acknowledgement of the compliment, but her eyes were gleaming greedily. "So would you say that the money will be doubled?"

Obadiah bowed again. "I am almost certain that this will be the case. But now I must hurry away to make the necessary arrangements. Of course—" he gave Mrs Haddington a hopeful glance— "were there to be any additional donations, that would be of enormous benefit."

Mrs Haddington nodded. "There might well be, Obadiah. I had a number of notes of promise, and not all of them have been placed at the bank. Perhaps another three or four guineas?"

"Excellent!" The Reverend was delighted. "And all for the good of the poor and afflicted."

He hesitated. "And that evil girl Minnie O'Sullivan is safely constrained?"

"Indeed she is." Mrs Haddington sounded so certain that Obadiah relaxed a little. "She has already given more than enough evidence of a shocking temper. She is working in the kitchen, and will be treated with the utmost severity until she learns obedience."

"Most satisfactory." The reverend gentleman bowed one last time, and Mrs Haddington rang for the butler to show him to the door.

As he left, she rubbed her hands together in glee; her decision to take to charitable works was proving to be a wise one. Philanthropy was already rewarding her with a more than generous income and, thanks to Obadiah Marpike, was likely to provide her with a substantial fortune in the not-too-distant future.

While the occasional sum would, of course, have to be bestowed upon Haddington Hall, by far the greater part could be absorbed by that most worthy of charitable causes – Honoria Haddington … but this was a fact best kept secret. She gazed out of the window at Obadiah's departing form, and sighed happily.

Mrs Haddington felt that she deserved a treat: a reward for all her hard work. A trip to London, perhaps? Or a new gown … or even both?

Honoria Haddington was not alone in having a secret. On leaving Mrs Haddington's elegant residence, the Reverend Obadiah Marpike took himself to a small and frowsty little shop that was so shy about its contents that it had no external sign at all.

His journey there was on foot, and anyone observing him would have been intrigued by the roundabout route that he chose, and by the number of times he glanced over his shoulder. He had the look of a furtive fox that has heard the hounds in the distance, and at all times he chose the shaded side of the street.

When a policeman appeared at the end of the road, he doubled back on himself and ducked into a side alley. *Take no chances*, he told himself.

Once inside the shop, he met a bespectacled man who greeted him as if they had met before. "The landed property you were considering in the New World, sir? The owner is willing to sell, if you can pay the price."

"I foresee no problem," Obadiah said. "The money is even now in my private account, and I paid in another fourteen guineas today with a further three or four to follow. I believe there is a steamship leaving from Liverpool quite soon; that will suit my plans most excellently well."

And with a decisive nod, he left the shop.

Ten

REMEMBERING THE REVEREND GENTLE-MAN'S compliments, Mrs Haddington sat back in her carriage and reflected on her life. Her income was now respectable in quantity, if not in origin, and a handsome clergyman was her close companion and aide.

She gave Edith a patronizing smile. "My dear, the last two orphans will be joining us at Haddington Hall today. Roland is even now on his way to collect them."

"And you say that they're sisters?" Edith asked.

"Indeed: 'Cissy' and 'Sal'. They've been living in a gin palace with a drunken old woman they say is their grandmother." Mrs Haddington gave a delicate shudder. "I imagine she's no relation at all. They had no papers to prove it – nothing.

They come from the same area of Middle-minster as Peg and Molly, as it happens. It will be delightful to see our happy band all together."

Edith noticed there was no mention of Minnie, and stifled a small sigh. It was all too obvious that Mrs Haddington had taken the reverend's instructions to heart, and was determined to make Minnie suffer for the supposed attack. As Mrs Krick opened the front door, a sense of gloom and depression settled around Edith like a dark cloud.

Mrs Haddington swooped into the narrow hall like a ship in full sail. "Is everything satisfactory?" she asked. "And have the new girls arrived yet?"

"No, Ma'am." Mrs Krick did not look sorry to be the bearer of bad news. "And those two upstairs, they won't come down."

"I see." Mrs Haddington frowned. "I shall speak to them. And where is Nellie?"

This was a sore point. Mrs Krick, having made Nellie welcome with tea and gossip, had been outraged to discover that the erstwhile parlour maid had been speaking no more than the truth when she said she intended to make the most of her new situation, and to work as little as possible.

So far there had been no sign of her; Mrs Krick had maliciously decided not to wake her, so that Mrs Haddington could discover this failing for herself.

"Not to put too fine a point upon it, Ma'am, Nellie is still lying in her bed."

Mrs Haddington's frown deepened. "Wake her at once! She has work to do."

"Certainly, Ma'am. I'll send Mangle." Mrs Krick, with a satisfied air, retired back to the kitchen. "Mangle? You're to wake Nellie."

Minnie, her arms aching from washing the kitchen floor, looked up from her mop and bucket. "Now?" she asked.

"What do you think, stupid girl? Of course now." Mrs Krick snapped. "Mrs Haddington's waiting for her: put that mop down, and hurry."

"Where's her room?" Minnie asked, and the housekeeper pointed. "Back stairs. Second door."

Unwillingly, but knowing that she would be shouted at if she didn't obey, Minnie made her way up the back stairs and knocked on Nellie's door.

There was no answer, so she knocked again, more loudly – and the door was flung open to reveal Nellie in nightgown and curlers.

"What do you want?" Nellie's expression was not welcoming.

"You got to get downstairs," Minnie told her. "Mrs Haddington's waiting for you."

Nellie scowled. "That old crone, Krick. She said as she'd wake me. Trying to get me into trouble, I bet."

Struck by a thought, she seized Minnie by the arm and pulled her inside her room.

"Listen here." She gave Minnie a cunning wink. "I knows as we didn't make the best of friends yesterday … but I got an idea. You and me, we could come to an arrangement."

Startled, Minnie stared at Nellie. "What sort of arrangement?"

Nellie lowered her voice. "I ain't here for the love of it, and I don't get paid more than what would feed a cat. So … if I sees something I likes, I reckon as it's fair enough if I takes it. You help me, you being a thief and all, and I'll see you right. Make sure as you get nice food. What do you say?"

Minnie had been listening with growing horror. Who did this young woman think she was? A red-hot wave of fury engulfed her, and she stamped her foot.

"I never thieved nothing! And I ain't about to start now – not for you, not for anyone." With a violent wrench of her arm, Minnie broke free and stormed back down the stairs, her heart thumping angrily.

Nellie's face was not pleasant as she looked after Minnie.

"So that's the way she wants to play it, is it?" she muttered. "Well … she'll be sorry. I'll make her wish she'd never been born."

Minnie, her face still flushed, hurtled through the kitchen and into the scullery, slamming the door behind her.

Mrs Krick raised her eyebrows. "Dangerous," she said to herself, and taking a rolling pin out of a drawer, she placed it where it could be reached at any time.

Mrs Haddington and Edith had heard nothing from the kitchen. Mrs Haddington was watching the driveway from the hallway window, and

Edith joined her as she recognized the sound of an approaching carriage.

"That will be Roland," Mrs Haddington remarked. "And about time too!"

Once again, the front door was heaved open, and the manservant appeared, a girl on either side of him.

"Did as I was told, Ma'am. Brought you the girls. And a fair amount of trouble it was, too."

"Really?" Mrs Haddington's eyebrows were raised. "And why was that?"

Roland shrugged. "Old hag shrieked and yelled – said she'd changed her mind, and didn't want them to leave after all. I threw her into her gin shop and brought the girls here."

"Thank you, Roland, you may go." Mrs Haddington dismissed him with a brisk nod, and turned to the girls.

Edith had been studying them, and saw that although they were dressed in the shabbiest of dresses, and the shawls round their shoulders were worn to threads, some attempt had been made to smarten them a little. The taller girl had a cherry-red ribbon in her hair, and the smaller a green one.

Maybe they could be friends with Minnie? she wondered. *She could do with a friend here.*

The sisters stood close together and, as Mrs Haddington approached them, arms outstretched in welcome, the smaller girl backed away.

"This ain't the right place," she said. "Gran said we was going to live in luxury."

She looked at the dark walls and the cracked and yellowed ceiling with an expression of deep disgust.

"This here's a dump. Gran said we was going to better ourselves, didn't she, Cissy? This ain't nothing like better. It's worser."

Cissy shook her head at her sister. "Don't you cause trouble, Sal. We ain't seen nothing yet." She gave Mrs Haddington a sycophantic smile. "Take no notice of her, Miss. She don't mean it."

"Yes, I does!" Sal stamped her foot. "Gran, she promised! She said we'd have a nice, bright house with big windows... Not like this. What's more, we're miles and miles and miles away from anywhere."

"What did I tell you?" Cissy nudged Sal with her elbow. "Shut it." She gave an apologetic cough. "Sorry about Sal. Our gran – she's been filling her head with rubbish. We're ever so happy to be here, and there's no two ways about it."

Mrs Haddington was delighted. "My dear! You're most welcome!"

Once again, Sal was nudged. "Hear that, Sal? We're welcome here." Cissy paused, and gave her benefactor a questioning glance. "And we get new clothes, and all of that? And meals? Gran, she said there'd be meals, regular. Good ones, too." She smacked her lips together. "I likes eating, I does. Gran, she never fed us nothing."

Sal scowled at her sister. "She did what she could. Don't you go telling fibs about—"

She never got to finish her sentence, as her sister clapped her hand over her mouth. "Give it a chance, Sal – we ain't been here but five minutes... OW!"

Sal had bitten her sister's hand. Before Cissy could retaliate, Mrs Haddington moved swiftly between them.

"Now, now, girls, let's not quarrel. Miss Lavingley will take you upstairs to the dormitory and show you your new clothes."

Edith noticed the younger sister was inspecting her silver bracelets with intense interest. When

Sal saw Edith looking, she immediately assumed an expression of injured innocence.

"What you staring at?" Her voice was a plaintive whine. "I ain't done nothing wrong. Think you're better than us, do you? Well, you ain't, and that's a fact." And she spat neatly on the floor, missing Edith's foot by inches.

Edith jumped back with an exclamation.

Cissy lunged at her sister, but was held back by Mrs Haddington.

"*Tchah!* Miss Lavingley's here to help you!"

"Who said as we wanted to be helped?" Sal was not to be mollified. "We been told lies. Big windows, sunny rooms, nice food to make us grow proper. That's what I wants!"

There was a shuffling noise, and Mrs Krick appeared. There was no sign of Gobbler, or of Minnie; Edith tried to see into the kitchen, but Mrs Krick had shut the door firmly behind her.

"Were you wanting luncheon, Ma'am?"

Both Cissy and Sal looked hopeful, and Mrs Haddington gave Mrs Krick a gracious smile. "What can you offer us, Mrs Krick?"

"There's pork, Ma'am. And greens from the garden."

The sisters looked at each other in mutual agreement. "Don't eat greens."

"Pork will do very well." Mrs Haddington was beginning to sound irritated. "Miss Lavingley, please take Cissy and Sal upstairs. Introduce them to Peg and Molly while you're there."

Peg and Molly had gone back to bed after breakfast. When Edith came into the dormitory with her two companions, they emerged, blinking, from under their blankets and stared at her.

"Why, if it ain't Miss Goody Two Shoes again," Peg said, and then, seeing Cissy and Sal, she sat bolt upright. "Them's the girls from the gin shop," she said. "What're you doing here?"

Cissy glared at her. "And you two was working in Babbel Lane, with that old clothes seller. Got thrown out, didn't you?"

Peg laughed. "Found a sixpence in a coat pocket," she said, "so we kept it, didn't we? Serves the old skinflint right."

Molly nodded. "Never paid us proper."

Sal was looking round, and it was evident that she wasn't impressed. "What's this place, anyway?" she demanded, as she took in the three empty beds. "We meant to sleep here? Well, I ain't going to, and that's that."

Edith, worried the atmosphere was becoming explosive, picked up one of the stripy dresses from the heap on the floor. "These are for you. Why don't you try one on?"

Cissy snatched it up and inspected it before slipping it over her head. She flounced round the room, waving her arms.

"Ooooh! Ain't I smart?"

Sal stuck out her tongue. "Stupid, more like."

"Better than rags," Cissy said. She fingered the material. "Made to last. Sell for a bit, this would."

This made Sal change her mind, and she, too, picked up a dress. When she was attired in waspish stripes, like her sister, Edith offered the two of them aprons – and was refused with a scornful, "We ain't no skivvies."

Peg had lost interest in the new arrivals. She was sniffing the air.

"I ain't half hungry. That our dinner on the go downstairs?" Giving Edith a piercing look, she added, "You, Miss Goody-Goody! Make yourself useful and go and see where that dog is. Moll and me, we're not moving if it ain't shut away."

"Dog?" Cissy swung round. "What dog?"

"Dirty big monster with great big teeth," Peg said, and Molly nodded her agreement.

Sal folded her arms. "Well, we ain't coming neither. Don't like dogs. Never did."

Edith, pleased to escape, made no comment. She hurried down the stairs, and found Mrs Haddington and Mrs Krick in the dining room, overseeing the arrangements for lunch.

A somewhat subdued Nellie was laying the table. Edith guessed that the parlour maid had been told in no uncertain terms how her employer felt about her failure to get up that morning.

"Is Gobbler to be kept in the kitchen?" she asked. "Only the girls say that they won't come down unless he's shut up."

Mrs Haddington was trying hard to suppress her anger. Nellie's behaviour had infuriated her, but so had that of the girls.

Nellie, banging plates down on the table, was within a hair's breadth of throwing them at her employer. Only the thought that she could take her feelings out on Minnie later prevented her. Now, seeing a chance to regain Mrs Haddington's favour, she said, "I'll go and fetch the girls down, Ma'am." She gave Edith a look of withering scorn. "I won't stand for none of their nonsense."

"Do, Nellie." Mrs Haddington sank down in a chair, exhausted by her charitable works. "Edith, dear – we'll leave Nellie to it, I think."

Edith had been trying hard to think of a way of getting to see Minnie before she left the house. Knowing that her mother's name had a magical effect on her companion, she smiled as brightly as she could.

"Of course, Mrs Haddington. But might I see the kitchen before we go? My mother specifically asked me to tell her about the kitchen." Having told one fib, Edith decided there was no harm in elaborating a little more. "Lady Lavingley is so interested in kitchens!"

Mrs Haddington beamed. "Mrs Krick, please show Miss Lavingley the kitchen."

"Thank you. I know the way," Edith said, and before either woman could stop her, she was hurrying down the passage.

Thoughts of Gobbler made her pause at the door, but her concern for Minnie overrode her fears and she lifted the latch and went in.

Eleven

AT FIRST EDITH THOUGHT THE KITCHEN was empty, but a sob from the scullery sent her running to look.

There she found Minnie, once again surrounded by dirty pots and pans, and with a heap of muddy vegetables in a basket on the floor beside her.

Even though there were still tears on her cheeks, she greeted Edith with a smile. "Morning, Miss. Or is it afternoon? All gets to feel the same in here."

"Minnie!" Edith looked at her with concern. "Why are you crying?"

Minnie shrugged. "Bit of a fight with that Nellie. She called me a thief, and I ain't taking that, not from no one."

Edith put out her hand to comfort Minnie, and immediately there was a fierce growl. Looking down, she saw Gobbler staring at her with deep suspicion.

Minnie giggled, and bent to pull his ears. "Him and me, we're friends now, Miss. He helps me with the pans."

"Minnie—" Edith gave a quick glance over her shoulder to make sure she wasn't overheard. "Minnie, I'm going to try and see the man who lied about you – the man who sent you here! He's a churchman: he must have some feelings." She shook her head. "People do and say things they don't mean when they're angry, and then they're sorry afterwards."

"Oh, Miss..." Minnie stopped. "It won't do no good, Miss. Truly. But it's nice of you to think of me."

Edith was not to be put off. "Was anyone else there when he slapped you?" she asked. "Anyone at all?"

Minnie rubbed her nose while she considered. "The housekeeper... I reckon she was standing by the door. But, Miss – he pays her! You don't tell tales on someone paying you money."

There was no time for a reply. Mrs Krick had come shuffling into the kitchen, and Edith, hurrying out of the scullery, was forced to pretend she was studying the curious arrangement of iron pipes above the ancient range.

The housekeeper immediately launched into a description of the range's various inadequacies and idiosyncrasies. Edith nodded and pretended to be listening, while she thought about what Minnie had told her.

Thumping feet and the sound of raised voices announced the arrival of the girls into the dining room for their lunch. Gobbler flattened his ears and growled deep in his throat, and before Minnie could soothe him into silence, Mrs Krick kicked him so hard that he whimpered.

Minnie's eyes blazed.

"Leave him be!" she shouted. "He didn't do nothing but growl, and that's what you want him to do, ain't it?"

Mrs Krick went purple. Rushing at Minnie, she pushed her back into the scullery, and slammed the door. Then, fishing in her apron pocket, she pulled out a key and turned it in the lock. "That'll teach her! Answering back and rage, rage, rage – that's all I've had from her."

Mrs Haddington, hearing sounds of conflict, came bustling into the kitchen. Mrs Krick launched into a highly biased account of Minnie's sins; Edith's attempt to justify her actions was brushed aside.

"If you ask me, Ma'am, the girl should stay under lock and key for the rest of the day! She should have been put in jail for what she did to the reverend gent, not sent here to cause trouble."

She banged the rolling pin on the table by way of punctuation.

"Indeed, Mrs Krick." Mrs Haddington nodded her agreement. "Leave her there as long as you think necessary. But we mustn't allow her bad behaviour to disrupt us; the girls are waiting for their meal. Edith, dear, my carriage is outside. I think we have seen quite enough for now. I have letters to write; perhaps you might consider assisting me this afternoon?"

Once in the carriage, and rolling away from Haddington Hall, Edith was silent. *I have to get Minnie out of that place,* she thought. *She said the housekeeper was there when she was slapped ... so there's a witness to what happened. I should go and see her.*

Mrs Haddington leant forward. "A penny for your thoughts, dear!"

Edith, taken by surprise, could only think to ask, "I was wondering: when do the girls begin their training? What will they learn?"

"Housekeeping skills and basic needlework." Mrs Haddington spoke without her usual enthusiasm; she was beginning to believe that she had made a mistake in choosing Nellie as the resident household tutor. She had seen another side of the parlour maid that morning, and she was gravely disappointed.

"I never liked needlework much," Edith said, "but I suppose it will come in useful." Then, seeing that Mrs Haddington seemed to be in an amicable frame of mind, she added, "Maybe Minnie could help teach some of the housekeeping skills? After all, her mother is a washerwoman—?"

"Certainly not." The philanthropist's expression changed. "That girl is to be worked hard and denied all privileges until she learns complete obedience. You read the Reverend Obadiah Marpike's letter, my dear. Minnie O'Sullivan is a vicious, evil girl."

She gave Edith a suspicious glance.

"What, exactly, has she been telling you?"

Edith frowned. "She told me she didn't mean to upset the table, and break the bottle of ink. It was an accident—"

"Stop!" Mrs Haddington held up an imperious hand. "As I thought. The girl has been lying to you, and lying outrageously. My dear Miss Lavingley, you have much to learn."

She gave a world-weary sigh.

"You are young, and your nature is sweet and trusting. I, on the other hand, am a mature gentlewoman ... and the reverend is a man of integrity. When he says that Mangle attacked him without cause or reason, you can be sure that he is telling the truth."

"But he *slapped* her!" Edith, indignant, spoke without thinking.

Mrs Haddington gasped, and fell back in her seat, fanning herself furiously with her gloves. "No, no, no, NO. Are there no depths to which that girl will not sink? Oh, the wickedness... The unadulterated evil. I cannot keep such a creature in my house, spreading poison like – like a snake. She must go before the law! Prison: *that's* the place for her."

Edith's heart was thumping wildly. She had been brought up to be respectful to those older than herself, but this was more than she could stand. "But she hasn't done anything to deserve going to prison – she was slapped! It was an accident!"

Mrs Haddington forgot all about Edith's mother, her dear friend Lady Lavingley. She was trembling with anger as she glared at Edith, her face a livid scarlet and her eyes bulging.

"Do you doubt my word? How can you possibly believe a guttersnipe like Mangle? A silly, ignorant child like you... You know nothing. Nothing at all!"

A terrible, cold anger consumed Edith.

"I'm afraid I disagree with you completely, Mrs Haddington – so please excuse me from any further association with your so-called charity. I wish you well."

She banged on the roof of the carriage.

"Stop! Stop!"

As they came to a sudden halt, Edith, her head held high, wrenched open the door and climbed out – and Mrs Haddington was left open-mouthed and staring.

Twelve

ONCE SHE HAD SLAMMED THE CARRIAGE door behind her, Edith, still trembling with indignation, looked around to see where she was. There was a familiar feel to the houses and shops, and she was certain that she had been to the milliners at one time or another … but which way should she go to get home?

Cabs and carriages and horse-drawn omni-buses filled the street, and Edith was jostled by other pedestrians as she hesitantly made her way towards a bow-windowed emporium that she thought she recognized. A small boy tugged at her sleeve and asked for a penny, and she made the mistake of taking her purse from her pocket; at once she was surrounded by children of all ages, begging for money and pulling at her dress.

"Oh … I wish I could help you, but I can't!" she said, but there was so much noise that her words went unheard.

The shrill cries grew louder, and a small hand grabbed at her purse and tweaked it from her grip. In a moment the lad was off, running like the wind, with other children in hot pursuit behind him.

Edith, shaken but also angry with herself for being so foolish, pulled her shawl closely round her as she tried to decide what to do next.

"Miss! Excuse me…"

The voice in her ear made her jump and turn in alarm, expecting to be robbed again; the tall boy behind her hastily stepped back when he saw her fierce expression.

"I ain't going to hurt you, Miss, honest!"

And he held out his hands to show he wasn't carrying any kind of weapon, and smiled such a cheerful smile that Edith couldn't help but smile back.

"I saw them boys rob you, Miss. Little varmints, they is!"

He shook his head in the manner of an aged and judgemental grandfather, amusing Edith even in the midst of her annoyance at being so easily deprived of her few coins.

"So – here you are, Miss." And with the air of a conjuror producing a rabbit from a hat, he handed Edith her purse from the depths of his coat pocket.

Edith looked at her rescuer with interest as she thanked him: there was an air of polite formality about him.

He gave her a small bow before asking, "Might you be a bit out of the right road, Miss?"

"I don't really know where I am," Edith confessed.

She was trying to make up her mind. Should she trust this boy, and ask him to show her the way home? After all, he had brought her purse back ... but could that have been a ruse?

The boy read her mind. "My name's Enry, Miss. Enry Potter. And if you wants a reference, the housekeeper at the Dog and Duck will tell you I'm able."

The name caught Edith's attention. "The Dog and Duck?"

"You knows the Dog, Miss?" A doubtful look crossed Enry's face. "Are you sure? The Dog and Duck at the end of Pocket Street?"

"Yes!" Edith's eyes shone as a glorious idea came to her. She clutched Enry's arm. "Will you take me there? Now? There's someone I need to talk to!"

Enry blinked. "If you say so, Miss." He shifted uncomfortably, and then said, "Miss – you was the one talking to Minnie in that Haddington Hall place, wasn't you?"

When Edith looked at him in astonishment, he went on, "I been keeping an eye on it. Went over there this morning, but there weren't no sign of Min, so I followed your carriage back. I ain't meaning no harm, Miss – not at all – but I was wondering, if you don't mind me asking … what was you doing there?"

Edith clapped her hands. "Oh! I'm so glad you followed me!"

She looked cautiously round as if she was expecting Mrs Haddington to be listening, then leant towards Enry.

"Isn't Haddington Hall just dreadful?" And when Enry nodded: "I'm desperate to get Minnie out of there. I know she never attacked anyone – she told me – but nobody will believe her. So, are you a friend of hers?"

Enry nodded. "Yes, Miss. Known her for years. And her family too."

"Then we'll rescue her together." Edith took his arm. "And the first thing is to talk to the Reverend Obadiah Marpike. I'm sure he must have made a mistake, and if I – I mean, *we* – can persuade him to say so, then that appalling Mrs Haddington will have to let Minnie go."

"He ain't the nicest gent, Miss." Enry was twisting his raw-knuckled fingers together as he tried to warn Edith. "He thinks everyone is out to do him down, and he gets in terrible tempers, and there ain't no talking to him reasonable like. I never yet heard him say sorry, not ever."

"But we have to try." Edith was determined. "And I want to talk to the housekeeper as well. Minnie said she might have seen what happened."

Enry's head was spinning. He knew that it was only Obadiah Marpike's two guineas a week that kept the Dog and Duck from financial ruin. Two guineas bought a lot of silence, and a refusal to see what was happening right under one's nose.

"Maybe, Miss…"

"So shall we go now?" Edith's voice was eager, and Enry, unable to think of any further reasons that might persuade her to give up her plan, nodded again.

Enry and Edith made a curious pair as they walked along, and several passers-by stopped to stare. Edith, dressed in the height of fashion, was arm in arm with a boy in rags and tatters, and she was talking to him in the most animated way.

As they turned the corner into Main Street, they were laughing together, much to the astonishment of an elderly woman in a particularly fine carriage. She called to her coachman to stop so she could raise her lorgnette and make sure that what she was seeing was not a figment of her imagination; then, with a tightening of her aristocratic lips, she ordered the horses to continue on their way.

"Lady Lavingley would *not* be happy if she could see this!" she remarked to her companion. "Really! What can the girl be thinking of? Absolutely shocking. I feel it to be nothing less than my duty to inform her mother. I will send Lady Lavingley a note!"

* * *

Edith, happily unaware that she had been observed, continued to chat to Enry as they walked. He was becoming more and more dazzled by her brightness and her positive view of the world, and also by her determination to help Minnie.

"I've read so many books," Edith told him, "and in every single one the villain is persuaded to admit to his guilt, and to swear that in the future he'll stick to the path of righteousness. It happens over and over again. Of course, sometimes it takes quite a lot of persuasion for them to see the error of their ways, but it should be easy with a man of the church, don't you think? After all, he must know all about forgiveness and being sorry for a mistake."

After half an hour of Edith's company, Enry could almost persuade himself that there was a possibility that Obadiah might agree that he had been mistaken.

But his doubts began to creep back as they approached the Dog and Duck. Even the windows had a disbelieving look about them, and Enry's footsteps slowed.

"You sure about this, Miss?"

Edith laughed, as much to persuade herself that all would be well as to reassure Enry.

"I've been thinking about it a lot. When Mother and I go to church, they're always talking about mercy. You wouldn't believe the number of sermons I've heard about it! It's one of the most important things ever."

Enry was far from convinced by this argument, but all he said was, "Yes, Miss. Here's hoping you're right."

"You will come in with me, won't you?" Edith asked. "You can tell him how miserable Minnie is, and how she's got a family and isn't an orphan at all, so she *shouldn't* be kept from them."

Enry gasped. "Me, Miss? He wouldn't let me in the room! Folks like him don't go talking to the likes of me. Well … not unless they wants their boots cleaned, or a message run, or their horses held. And that ain't talking. That's ordering."

"Oh." Edith looked at her companion, and her expression was very serious. "Why shouldn't you be able to talk to the same people that I can? Doesn't it make you angry?"

In Enry's experience life was always unfair, but that was the way things were, and always had been. He stood still while he considered this, until Edith pulled at his arm.

"So ... are we going inside?"

"Oh – yes, Miss." Enry opened the door, and stood back to let her go into the kitchen. The housekeeper, peeling potatoes, looked up in surprise at the sight of an elegantly dressed girl walking through the door.

"Excuse me, Miss, but you must have made a mistake: this isn't any kind of place for a young lady like you." And then, seeing Enry, she said sharply, "Enry Potter! What were you thinking of? Bringing the quality into my kitchen... And where have you been? I need you for errands."

Edith stepped forward, holding out her hand. "I'm sorry. I asked Enry to bring me here – it's not his fault. I'd like to speak to the Reverend Obadiah Marpike, if I may."

"The Reverend?" The housekeeper was startled.

"That's right." Edith drew herself up to her full height. "It's an important matter to do with the Literary Ladies' Charitable Association for Orphans. My name is Edith Lavingley." And then, remembering that it was her mother who had been approached by Mrs Haddington, she added, "My mother is *Lady* Lavingley."

There was just enough authority in Edith's voice to make the housekeeper take her seriously.

She gave Edith a respectful nod, and said, "If you don't mind waiting here, Miss, I'll go and see if the Reverend is happy to see you."

And she hurried out of the kitchen.

Edith looked at Enry. "Do you think I should follow her?"

Enry pulled at his ear in perplexity, but before he could make a decision, Edith took matters into her own hands.

She was doing her best to hide the fact that she was nervous, but she had a strong suspicion that if she didn't act quickly, she wouldn't feel brave enough to do anything at all to save Minnie. She straightened her bonnet and whisked after the housekeeper, and was just in time to see her going into what was, presumably, Reverend Obadiah Marpike's room.

The door was left open. Edith was on the point of following when she heard her name, and paused to listen.

A moment later, her eyes opened very wide …

and Edith hastily gathered up her skirts and fled back to the kitchen.

Once there, she threw herself onto a chair, and did her best to look as if she hadn't moved.

Thirteen

IF MRS KRICK HAD HOPED MINNIE WOULD calm down as a result of being locked in the scullery, she was mistaken. When Nellie finally unlocked the door several hours later, she was still simmering with rage.

Nellie had intended to give Minnie a hard slap as a sign of her personal disapproval; she was dissuaded from this, however, by the presence of Gobbler, who greeted Minnie with quivering delight while simultaneously growling darkly at her would-be attacker and showing his teeth.

Backing hastily away, Nellie said, "You're wanted upstairs. Bring a mop and bucket. I want those floors cleaned before the girls go to bed, and when I says 'clean', I means it. I'll be watching you, every minute. And hurry up about it!"

As Minnie filled the bucket with water and went to find the mop, Nellie took herself up to the dormitory where Peg, Molly, Cissy and Sal were sitting in a row on one of the beds, and whispering to each other.

They had bonded over the discovery that they loathed Mrs Haddington, and had been trying to outdo each other in calling her names.

"She's a hornswoggling hag," Peg offered.

Molly giggled. "I likes that! Hornswoggling hag-bag!"

"More of a rubbishy ratbag," Cissy suggested, and it was Sal's turn to giggle.

"She's a wailing whooperup," said Sal, looking pleased with herself. "All noise and nothing good."

They fell silent as soon as Nellie appeared, and looked at her with suspicion: was she a spy for Mrs Haddington? It seemed she had some kind of role in the house, but it hadn't been made clear to them what exactly this was.

Nellie gave the girls a sly wink. "Planning and plotting?" she asked.

Peg, Molly and Sal looked doubtfully at her, but Cissy chuckled. "Got to look out for number one." She fingered her dress. "Going to sell this, soon as I gets out of here."

Sal nodded at Nellie. "Me too." She looked round the gloomy dormitory, with its dark and dusty rafters and rough wooden floors. "We was promised big windows. Gran said we was going to better ourselves, and me and Cissy, we're going back—"

"Shut it!" Cissy clamped a hand over her sister's mouth. Although Nellie appeared friendly, Cissy knew enough of the world to be suspicious of anyone in a position of authority, however minimal that authority might be. They were always happy to use information to their own advantage.

Nellie gave Cissy a knowing nod. "It's all right: I won't tell her high and mightiness. Not blooming likely! Now, d'you want some fun?"

Peg and Molly sat up. "Fun?"

Nellie nodded, and pointed to the door as Minnie, laden down with the heavy bucket, came staggering in.

"This here's called Mangle. Watch her! She's got a temper like a raging bull ... but she's here to work. Ain't that right, Mangle?"

Minnie, her lips pressed tightly together, nodded. She knew Nellie was trying to make her angry, and she was doing her best not to rise to her taunting – but it was hard.

"Shocking awful, she is." Nellie went on. She grinned at the girls. "Mangle, she hit a poor innocent man – a man of the church, would you ever believe it? Nearly killed him, by all accounts. I'm right, ain't I, Mangle?"

Peg gave a cautious chuckle and Molly, hearing her, did the same. Cissy sat back on the bed to see what would happen next, while Sal watched Minnie cheerfully, enjoying her struggle to keep calm.

Minnie's knuckles were very white as she began to mop the floor. She made no answer to Nellie's accusation, and Nellie's eyes gleamed.

"See? She ain't denying it. Proper bad 'un, she is." She pointed under a bed. "You missed a bit."

Sal shuddered. "I ain't sleeping in no muck heap. Our gran, she said— Ooof!" Once again she was silenced by Cissy.

"If you mentions them windows one more time, I'm putting you out through one," she threatened.

Nellie, irritated by the interruption, brought their attention back to Minnie. "You ain't listening to me! Move that bed."

With an angry wrench, Minnie pulled the iron bed away from the wall, and whirled her mop over the bare boards.

Don't answer back, she told herself. *Don't answer back. It'll make things worse.*

"Now that bed there," Nellie instructed. "Blimey! Ain't you never done mopping before?"

Minnie heaved furiously at the second bed, dislodging an unfortunate spider, who scuttled across the floor.

Sal screamed, but Nellie, with a grin, picked it up and squeezed it between her finger and thumb.

"Won't be walking round at night now," she said in satisfied tones, and wiped her fingers on the back of Minnie's dress. "Oooh, look. You got a stain on your nice new uniform – Mrs H, she won't like that."

Minnie bit her lip so hard that she tasted blood, but still she didn't answer.

Nellie, frustrated in her efforts, tried a different line of attack.

She winked at Sal, then said, "I reckon as Mangle weren't brought up proper. Bet her mam never taught her nothing... Bet her mam was always on the bottle and rolling drunk. Bet her mam—"

The rest of her remark was lost when Minnie picked up the bucket of dirty water and poured it over her tormentor's head.

As Nellie coughed and spluttered, Minnie dropped the mop and headed for the stairs.

"Stop her!" Nellie yelled, but all four girls were shouting with laughter, and not one made any attempt to do as she demanded.

Nellie, furiously wiping water from her eyes, plunged after Minnie, only to trip over the mop and fall flat on her face in a dirty puddle.

Sal and Molly became hysterical; they whooped and shrieked, and clutched each other in glee, while Peg and Cissy shook with uncontrollable mirth.

It was Nellie's turn to lose her temper: snatching up the mop, she turned on the girls and began to beat them round the shoulders, swearing horribly as she did so. Cissy swore back, but Sal leapt off the bed, grabbed Nellie's arm and bit it hard – just as Minnie, hurtling to the bottom of the stairs, collided with Mrs Krick carrying a tray of dirty crockery and the remains of her evening meal.

Gobbler, dashing out of the kitchen, added to the confusion by blundering into the housekeeper's legs as she staggered to and fro, and the teapot fell on his head as she crashed to the floor.

Gobbler howled, Mrs Krick screeched – and Minnie sped on into the kitchen, out of the back door and into the garden.

She scrambled over the fence and ran and ran until every breath was an agonizing knife thrust in her chest; on and on through the scrubby woodland, where a hidden root tripped her and she fell into a bed of old, dry leaves.

"Ooooof!"

Slowly she got her breath back. Gazing up through the branches to the late-afternoon sky above, she checked to see if she was all in one piece.

Finding she was only bruised, she sat up … and then lay down again. The leaves were soft, and she was comfortable, and very, very weary.

Every bone in her body ached, and her eyelids were so, so heavy…

By the time Gobbler finally tracked her down, Minnie was asleep. The dog sighed happily, licked her face and curled up beside her.

Fourteen

THE HOUSEKEEPER'S KNOCK ON THE Reverend Obadiah Marpike's door had been greeted with a growl, and the instruction, "Wait!" There was the sound of rustling papers, and then, "Come in!"

The housekeeper did as she was told. "If you please, Sir, there's a young lady here to see you. From a charity, Sir – the Middleminster Ladies, or some such."

"A young lady?" Obadiah Marpike raised his eyebrows. He had never met anyone other than Mrs Haddington from the Middleminster Literary Ladies, and he had no particular desire to widen his acquaintance. "Did she give a name?"

The housekeeper nodded. "She says her name is Miss Edith Lavingley."

"Lavingley? Lavingley... The name sounds familiar." Obadiah straightened the pens on his table as he searched his memory. "Why do I know that name?"

"Said her mother was a 'Lady Lavingley'," the housekeeper said helpfully, and Obadiah dropped his pens and stared at her.

"Lady Lavingley?" He swore loudly. "But she lives in Bath! How can she possibly be here in Middleminster?"

As the housekeeper looked at him in astonishment, he bent to pick up the scattered pens in order to cover his expression of extreme alarm.

When he stood up again, he had recovered sufficiently to be able to say, "Tell this 'Miss Lavingley' that I am about to go out – I have an urgent appointment! She must address any concerns she may have to Mrs Haddington; I am not the person she should be speaking to."

And he all but pushed the housekeeper out of the room, and slammed the door behind her.

On arriving back in the kitchen, the housekeeper explained with as much tact as she could that Obadiah was not available as he had an appointment elsewhere. She was relieved to find that Edith took the news without an argument.

"Please don't apologize," she said as she got to her feet. "I'm sure he's a very busy man, and I should leave you in peace." She hesitated, trying to think of the best way to ask about Minnie. "Might I ask … do you remember Minnie O'Sullivan coming here?"

"Yes I do, Miss." The housekeeper nodded. "Caused no end of upset, she did. But what's a girl like that to you, if I may be so bold as to ask?"

"I believe she has been punished most severely for something that wasn't her fault." Edith looked straight at the housekeeper. "And I don't think that's fair."

The housekeeper at the Dog and Duck was not a bad woman. She had seen everything that had taken place between Minnie and Obadiah, and had the odd moment when she had wondered if she should have defended the girl. All the same, two guineas a week was two guineas she could not afford to be without − and payment of that magnitude surely included discretion, as well as hot dinners.

Least said, soonest mended was a motto that had always served her well.

"Well," she said slowly, "I'd go as far as to allow the girl was provoked a little … but she had no business to go breaking ink bottles, and shouting at him. If you want my opinion, Miss, you'll leave well alone. Once the Reverend's got an idea that someone's done him wrong, you'll not shake it out of him."

"I see." Edith was still trying to make sense of what she had heard. "I thought he'd be more—" she tried to find the right word— "forgiving. I mean, he is a priest."

The housekeeper shrugged. "There's men of the church, and men of the church," she said. "And come to that, anyone can put on a clerical suit and collar, can't they? And who's to know the difference?"

Edith stared at her. "You're right. Who's to say that the 'Reverend' is even a real priest?"

"I never said anything like that." The housekeeper, already regretting having shared as much as she had, sounded flustered. "And don't you go saying I did, because I'll deny it to my dying day. He never misses paying his bill, and that's good enough for me. And I've got work to see to, Miss, if you'll excuse me."

Edith, recognizing the dismissal, looked at Enry, who was leaning against the wall. "Of course. Could Enry find me a hansom cab, do you think?"

"That he can," the housekeeper said. "Enry – you go with the young lady and make sure you find her a respectable driver. And when you've done that, come straight back. There's errands that need running, and laundry to collect."

As Edith and Enry reached the street outside, Edith seized Enry's arm. "Enry, the most remarkable thing happened when I was listening outside the Reverend Obadiah Marpike's room."

Enry looked blank. "Remarkable, Miss?"

"Yes!" Edith was alight with excitement. "He was sounding quite calm and ordinary, but as soon as he heard my mother's name, he changed. He was ever so annoyed that she didn't live in Bath, and he swore about it quite dreadfully! And that's strange, because she went to Bath after Father died to take the waters, but she's never lived there, and I've never once heard her mention him. He must have a secret … but what kind of secret? He's about to go out … we *have* to follow him."

"But—" Enry began, and Edith immediately apologized.

"I'm so sorry, I know you've got work to do. I can follow him! Oh…" The light went out of her eyes. "Actually, I can't – not if he takes an omnibus or a cab. I haven't enough money."

Enry considered the situation. He had never been paid by the housekeeper at the Dog and Duck. Free meals, and the occasional tip from a customer, were all he could expect; most of his meagre income came from holding horses, or sweeping roads when he had time.

He made his decision. "I'll do whatever I can, Miss: anything to help Minnie. I can run after him easy if he takes a four-wheeler … but you didn't ought to try any such thing." He paused, then said in his most grandfatherly tones, "Didn't you ought to be getting home, Miss?"

"Mother thinks I'm with Mrs Haddington," Edith told him. "But you're quite right: I can't run after anything. Oh … *why* do we girls have to be dressed up as if all we ever do is sit and sip tea?"

Enry shook his head. "I'm afraid I can't tell you that, Miss."

The boy's serious expression made Edith laugh.

"Tell me when you discover the answer," she said. "And you might be right about my going home; it was so very strange, the way the Reverend Obadiah Marpike reacted to my mother's name. I should go and find out if she knows him, shouldn't I? And you can find out where he's going, and then we can meet later and make a plan of action for what we do next."

Enry nodded. It seemed easier to agree, even though he wasn't entirely certain that he had followed Edith's thought process abou the reverend. "Whatever you say, Miss."

"I'm not sure if Mother will let me go out again on my own, now I come to think of it." Edith was still making plans. "I'm meant to be accompanied by a maid, or a companion ... so could you come to my house? Cook won't mind at all if we meet: I often escape to the kitchen when Mother's in one of her moods, and we make cake, or ginger biscuits. There's nothing like making ginger biscuits when your mother's being difficult."

"Sounds like a good idea to me, Miss," said Enry. "What time?"

"Mother always retires to her room about eight," Edith told him. "So any time after that. And I think it'll be easier if you come round to the back door." She sighed. "Harbottle disapproves of just about anyone who – who doesn't look quite like the usual caller."

Enry was mystified. "What bottle?"

"Harbottle." Edith sighed again. "He was Father's manservant in the army, and then when Father was killed, he came back home as a sort of butler. He opens the doors to visitors and is horribly fierce because he thinks he has to protect me and Mother, because Father isn't around any more. He's the kindest man ever, when you get to know him."

"I'll go round the back, Miss. I don't never go in the front door of the Dog and Duck, neither." Enry gave Edith a beaming smile. "Don't make no difference to me. Not at all."

"That's very kind of you, Enry." Edith was genuinely grateful. "And now … could you tell me which way to go to get home? Lavingley Hall, just off Salcome Street." She gave an exasperated

"Tchah!" before continuing, "Isn't it ridiculous that I can't find my own way?"

"It ain't too far, Miss. I'll make you a map." Enry pulled a piece of chalk out of his pocket and, using a handy door as his drawing board, showed Edith where to go.

"That's very clear," she said. "Thank you so much – and see you later." Then, with a wave of her hand, she was walking briskly away.

Enry looked after her, a worried expression on his face. *What if she gets into trouble again?*

But at that moment the door of the Dog and Duck opened, and Obadiah Marpike came hurrying out. Seeing Enry, he stopped.

"Fetch me a cab, and be quick about it! Twenty seven Kingston Row. Hurry, boy!"

Enry, hiding a triumphant grin, did as he was told. Fortunately for him, a cab driver was feeding his horse on the stand at the end of the street. After giving him his instructions, and waiting just long enough to see the cab rattling towards the Dog and Duck, Enry set off running after Edith.

Them wicked boys is everywhere, he told himself. *Pickpockets too ... and worser. I'll see as she gets home safe – and then it'll be a quick run to Twenty Seven Kingston Row!*

Fifteen

THE REVEREND OBADIAH MARPIKE TOOK out his watch for the seventh time, checked it and put it back in his pocket with a grunt of irritation. The cab was so slow that he was tempted to get out and walk; the following day was market day in Middleminster and already small carts heaped high with vegetables, barrows laden with cheeses, and boys with a goose under each arm were clogging Main Street as they made their way to the market square.

Obadiah leant out of the window to shout abuse at a woman who was chasing a chicken – the driver of the cab, hearing a shout but not what was said, immediately brought his horse to a halt. With a muttered curse, Obadiah flung open the door and stormed away.

"Oi! What about my shilling?" The driver was outraged, but Obadiah didn't care. Turning up his collar, and, wrapping his scarf around his face, he pushed his way past the woman and strode on along the road, using his stick and his elbows when necessary to force his way through the crowds.

Turning off Main Street, he found himself almost alone; increasing his pace, he strode to the end of the road, and swung into Kingston Row, once again checking his watch.

"Will he still be here? I must change my plans at once…" he muttered to himself. "I must hasten my departure. Lady Lavingley in Middleminster? Why? What can she be doing here? When I met her, she was taking the waters of Bath – she told me that she'd be living in the vicinity of Bath for a year or more. And sending her daughter to see me… Why would she do that, unless she had suspicions?"

Obadiah pulled the collar of his coat up even higher – a moment later, he had reached Number 27, and was knocking on the small dark door of the shop he had visited before. There was no answer, and he moved to look through the windows, but they were so dirty that it was impossible to see what was inside... And there was no light, so Obadiah could see no movement. Cursing fluently, he turned away to find a small child staring at him.

"He's gone home, Mister," she said. "I asked him for a penny, but he says, 'Get away, you little viper!' Proper mean, he is."

She gave Obadiah a hopeful look, but it had no effect other than to make him brush her out of his way as if she were nothing more than a shadow – and then, after a brief moment of indecision, he swung on his heel to go back the way he had come.

As he reached the end of Kingston Row, he checked his stride; did he know the boy swinging round the corner? A second glance showed him the boy was gone and, thinking he must have been mistaken, he marched onwards.

Enry, flattened against the wall, breathed out. "Gor blimey! I never expected that!" He watched the reverend gentleman's retreating back to make sure that he hadn't been recognized, then slipped into Kingston Row and began to count the numbers. On reaching Number 27, he, too, saw the small girl.

Giving her a beaming smile, he asked, "Know who lives here, do you?"

She looked up. "Got a penny?"

Fishing in his pockets, Enry produced a length of faded blue ribbon. "Ain't got no pennies, but you can have this. Pretty, like you!"

"Hmmmm." The girl eyed the ribbon as if assessing its value. Then, accepting it graciously, she said, "You don't want to mess with him in there. Deals in dirty money, and stuff like that."

"Dirty money?" Enry stared at her, and she shrugged.

"That's what her at the corner shop says: 'You gets all sorts knocking on his door, and none of them looks respectacle.'" She giggled. "All of them with their collars up and their hats pulled right down over their noses ... and they all peers over their shoulders afore they goes inside. Dead suspicious, they looks. Got any more ribbon?"

"No." Enry shook his head. "So where's this corner shop?"

The little girl indicated the far end of the street with a tip of her head. "Down there."

And then she was gone, waving her ribbon in the air as if it was a flag.

Enry smiled as he saw her disappear into a narrow alleyway, then he, too, tried to see if he could see anything through the window.

Rubbing at a pane with the corner of his coat, he cleared away enough dirt to make a spy hole. He was attempting to make out what the piles of books and papers inside might be, when a heavy hand landed on his collar and gripped it so tightly that Enry gasped for breath.

"And what do you think you're doing, peeking in through my windows?" The speaker was small but solidly built, and his deep-set eyes were steely cold behind his spectacles.

Enry, half strangled, still had enough wit to notice that his attacker was holding a bunch of keys. What could he say?

A wild thought came to him, and he gasped out, "I got a message, Mister! I got a message from the reverend gentleman... The Reverend Obadiah Marpike!"

The cold eyes peered closely at him. "Oh, yes? And why should I believe you?"

"Him as lives at the Dog and Duck, Mister!"

The grip on Enry's collar loosened, and he was able to breathe again as the man looked him up and down. "Got the money, has he?"

Enry blinked. Should he say yes, or no? He decided to compromise. "Says as he's nearly there. Still got a bit to collect." And he waited, butterflies in his stomach, to be told he was a fraud and a trickster.

Instead, the man grunted, and let him go. "Thought as much: tell him the seller won't wait more than a couple of days. There's another buyer interested, and he's got cash to spare." The man gave a contemptuous chuckle. "Plenty of folk wanting to take their dirty money away to the New World, where it can't be investigated – not that it's any of my business."

He gave Enry a chilly stare.

"Nor yours, neither, imp. Now get back to that reverend of yours, and tell him what I said. Another thirty guineas, and the deal's done."

He turned his back on Enry and, rattling his keys, opened the door of his shop.

"Yes, Mister, thank you, Mister, I'll be sure to tell him, Mister," Enry gabbled, and sped away. As he ran, he was thinking about what he had learned, and wondering what Edith would have to say.

"Dirty money... Ain't much like the kind of reverend she's used to, I'll be bound!"

Sixteen

L ADY LAVINGLEY WAS NEVER ANGRY. IT was well known that anger was bad for the complexion, and resulted in truly horrid lines and wrinkles that no amount of scented rose water could remove.

Nevertheless, her nostrils were pinched and white as she sat in her private sitting room waiting for Edith to return, a folded note in her clenched hand. It informed her that her daughter – her one and only daughter! – had been seen walking the streets of Middleminster with a ragamuffin of a boy ... a *street urchin*.

Lady Lavingley shuddered. Concerns for Edith's safety were far from her mind; her only thought was for her own reputation, and the reputation of the name of Lavingley.

How on Earth could Edith possibly make an advantageous marriage in a couple of years' time, if she had the reputation of a hoyden?

Edith, quite unaware of what was awaiting her, walked thoughtfully up the stairs to her mother's private sitting room. She was considering what she could say that wasn't too far from the truth … and at the same time, discover if the name of Obadiah Marpike meant anything to Lady Lavingley.

She was not in the least prepared to find her mother sitting bolt upright, quivering with self-righteous indignation.

"Edith, I find it impossible to even begin to express the depth of my displeasure. I have been reliably informed that you were seen today walking – *walking alone!* – with a revolting guttersnipe of a boy. I cannot imagine that you have any kind of excuse for this *abominable* behaviour, but I am prepared to listen to what you might wish to say to me by way of explanation."

If Lady Lavingley was expecting an apology from her daughter, she was mistaken. Until she met Mrs Haddington, Edith had been a quiet, obedient girl. But now, she had found friends.

Her eyes firing sparks, she glared at her mother as she said, "That was Enry, and he's no more a guttersnipe than I am! He saved me from being robbed – and not only did he *save* me, but he made sure that I got home safely."

Lady Lavingley's voice rose, and two red spots burned angrily on her pale cheeks.

"Do you have any idea how supremely selfishly you have behaved? We are in debt, Edith – deeply in debt. And these debts will engulf us completely unless you do your duty in two or three years' time, and marry well … but nobody in polite society will ever consider marrying a girl who runs around the streets."

Edith, equally as angry, leant forward, and banged her fist on the small table beside her mother's chair.

"And whose fault is it that we're in debt, Mother? What happened to darling Father's money? You've never told me what happened… Because it most certainly was none of *my* doing!"

For a moment it looked as if Lady Lavingley was about to scream. It was with an enormous effort that she controlled herself, and then, alarming Edith far more, she burst into hysterical sobs.

"Everything, but *everything*, turns to dust and ashes in my hands. Your father insists on going to war and getting himself killed, that dreadful Sir Oliver Mothercarp – who promised my investment would be doubled, redoubled and doubled again – disappears without a trace, leaving me all but penniless ... and now my only daughter is bringing me to the brink of ruin and despair."

The next moment Lady Lavingley was wildly ringing the bell, and when her maid came scurrying in, she demanded that Harbottle be sent for.

As soon as the butler appeared, she pointed to Edith. "Take her to her room, Harbottle – take her to her room, lock her in and bring me the key. At once, do you hear?"

Harbottle, his face impassive, bowed. "As you wish, m'lady."

And to Edith's horror, he seized her arm and marched her out of the room. Once outside, he lessened his grip, and shook his head sadly.

"I'm right sorry to have to do this, Miss – but orders is orders."

And the next thing Edith knew, she was in her bedroom, the key was turning in the lock ... and she was a prisoner.

She flew at the door and tugged and pulled at the handle, but the door was substantial, and the lock strong.

Scarlet with rage, Edith flung herself on her bed. *How dare she?* she thought. And then, *What do I do now?*

She jumped up and began to stride round and round her room, her thoughts buzzing in her head like angry wasps.

Gradually, she began to grow calmer, and her to mind to settle.

Enry will come round to the kitchen, and I won't be able to talk to him ... but maybe I can ask Harbottle to tell Cook to tell him that I'm locked in?

She ran to the bell, and pulled on the rope.

"Mother can't keep me here for ever," she told herself. "So tomorrow I'll pretend that I'm sorry ... although I'm not at all! But if apologizing gets me out of here, I'll do it, for Minnie's sake."

Thinking of Minnie reminded Edith of Obadiah Marpike, and she thumped her pillows in frustration.

"Oh, it's so annoying! I want to know if Enry discovered anything... And I never got to ask Mother if she recognized Obadiah's name."

She looked at the door.

"Surely Harbottle should have been here by now?"

But there was no Harbottle. Although Edith pulled on the bell rope over and over again, still no one came, and by the time her room had grown dark and cold, she realized that her summons would not be answered, and neither was she going to be given a lamp, or brought supper, or have her fire lit.

Trying hard not to burst into tears of hunger, fury and resentment, Edith climbed into bed.

I'll find Enry tomorrow, she told herself. *I just hope to goodness he doesn't think I deserted him...*

Enry wasn't entirely surprised when he was turned away from Edith's kitchen door.

The kitchen maid giggled when she saw him, and when he told her that Miss Edith had arranged to meet him in the kitchen, she giggled even more.

"*You?*" she said. "*You* meet Miss Edith? Go on, get away with you."

Enry tried his widest smile. "It's true! We was out together today." He considered how he could sound more convincing. "She was with that Mrs Haddington, and I met her after that."

This meant nothing to the kitchen maid, but the cook, wondering what was going on, had appeared behind her.

"And who might you be? If you're selling, we're not buying."

Recognizing the voice of authority, Enry ducked his head. "I'm Enry Potter, Ma'am. Miss Edith, she said I was to meet her here in your kitchen. Said you was always kind to her, and she made ginger biscuits and all with you."

To his surprise, this remark resulted in the cook pushing the kitchen maid back indoors.

Leaning forward, she said, "That does sound like my Miss Edith, so I'll tell you this for nothing. She's in trouble. Locked in her room. So whoever you are, she'll not be meeting you in my kitchen, or anywhere else."

And then the door was slammed shut, and Enry was alone again.

Locked in her room? He shook his head. *So what now?* An enormous yawn overcame him, and thoughts of his bed seemed suddenly very tempting. *I'll come back here tomorrow. Or I'll go and try to see Min...*

And, debating with himself as he went, Enry made his way back to the battered stable he called home.

Seventeen

AS ENRY WAS TUCKING HIMSELF UP IN AN old rug ready for sleep, Minnie, a long way away, had woken with a jolt. A warm furry body was snoring gently beside her, and for a brief moment she panicked – but as she sat up, Gobbler opened his eyes and gave her a welcoming lick.

"Gobbler," she said fondly. "You didn't ought to have followed me … but I'm ever so glad that you did."

As she hugged the dog, she was rewarded with a thump of his tail, and a friendly grunt.

"You're ever such a good doggie – but that Mrs Krick will be out on the hunt for you, sooner or later, and then we'll be in terrible trouble."

She yawned, and Gobble yawned too.

"Best leave that worry for the morning," Minnie told him, and Gobbler, with a weary sigh, put his head down on his paws.

The night sky was spattered with silver stars, and there was a cool breeze blowing, but Minnie didn't feel cold. She snuggled down in her leaves again, her arm over Gobbler's back, wondering what had woken her, and if she could get back to sleep—

Voices!

As Gobbler pricked up his ears and growled, Minnie sat bolt upright, her heart crashing against the walls of her chest.

Yes: she could hear voices. She jumped to her feet, but had no idea which way she should go; holding on to the trunk of her sheltering tree, she held her breath as she listened.

There was no doubt that someone was stamping heavily in between the trees and bushes. A dim and wavering light suggested that the traveller, or travellers – there was surely too much noise for a single person – had a lantern.

"Gor, Sal! It's like the blooming pits of hell in here! We gotta stop afore we kills ourselves!" Minnie suppressed a gasp of astonishment as she recognized this voice. Cissy! And Sal must be with her... But what could possibly have brought them to the woods in the middle of the night?

"What, is there bears? Does bears climb trees?" Sal sounded nervous.

There was a snort of laughter. "Ain't no bears. Anyways, bears is nothing like as bad as that place. Gor! My shoulders is hurting terrible! How's yours, Peg?"

There was a grunt. "Sore."

Minnie's thoughts whirled. So Peg was there, too? What about Molly? Had they all run away? Should she tell them she was there?

She moved behind the tree to give herself time to think, and as she did so, she trod on a dry stick. The snap was loud, and there was a piercing shriek, together with a crash and the disappearance of the light. This was followed by a trembling wail.

"Cissy? Peg? Moll? I can't see. I don't know where anyone is."

The answer was a furious hiss. "Shut your mouth! It's bad enough you dropped the candle, so shut up and listen ... listen for breathing."

Sal began to cry loud, terrified sobs.

"Bears – it's them bears, I knows it is! I want to go back, Cissy... I want to go back!"

"And what'll they do to us then? You bit that Nellie, remember? Bit her hard! Drew blood. And you whacked her with that mop – whacked her good and proper. They ain't going to give you roses for that, are they?"

Cissy was angry, but there was a note of uncertainty in her voice, and Sal went on sobbing.

"I'm scared, Ciss, I'm ever so scared."

"Ain't just you." Peg sounded far from comforting. "Me and Moll, we're scared witless – but we ain't making a blooming fuss and dance about it."

"Oi, leave Sal alone!" Cissy wasn't going to allow anyone else to attack her sister. That was her prerogative, and hers alone. "We got to do what we said we was going to do. We got to get back to our gran, and tell her there ain't no big windows, and nothing like we was promised."

"I loves Gran," Sal agreed. "She'll be ever so pleased if we comes back."

Minnie, listening with intense interest, crept nearer to hear better. A twiggy branch caught in her hair, and as she pulled herself free, it swished back against the tree trunk with a sharp slap. The girls screamed, and Minnie jumped.

"Oh God," she said, and then, realizing she had given herself away, "It's me. Minnie."

"Minnie?" Cissy sounded disbelieving, but Sal gave a hiccuping squeak of relief.

"We thought you was a bear!"

"Ain't seen no bears yet," Minnie said. "What are you doing here? You run away, too?"

Peg grunted. "Wasn't going to stay there no longer. That Nellie – she was mad!"

"That's right," Molly, Peg's echo, agreed. "Really mad!"

Cissy began to chuckle. "You half drowned her with that bucket, Min. As for old Krick, she was rolling on the floor with tea leaves in her hair, cussing and swearing worser than I ever heard. Laugh? We was wetting ourselves! So she turns on us and calls us all sorts ... so we legs it, and we ain't going back. Not never."

Minnie was thinking hard. It seemed that her actions had won the girls' respect, but she was shocked to hear what she had done.

They'll be after me now, more than ever, she told herself. She felt Gobbler pressing against her leg, and she put down a hand to stroke his ears for comfort.

"So how are we going to get out of here, Min?" Cissy asked. "I hate these trees! Can't see nothing, and there's all sorts of bugs and creepy things living in them, I'll be bound."

Minnie, surprised that she was being asked for advice, considered for a moment. "There's a whole heap of dry leaves here," she said. "I been asleep, and it was ever so comfy. We can't see nothing now, so why don't we wait until it gets light?"

"Don't see as we can do much else," Cissy agreed, and Peg grunted her agreement.

"A bit of shut-eye won't hurt nobody. Watch out, though. Moll − she snores like an old hog."

Molly's snores echoed through the long night hours, and Minnie lay awake wondering how Peg, Sal and Cissy could sleep so peacefully.

As the light gradually seeped through the trees and brought colour back to the wood, she saw that Cissy and Sal were wrapped in each other's arms, and a pang of terrible homesickness made her shut her eyes.

Oh, Bobs, she thought. *I ain't half missing you...*
Are you missing me? And Mam – my dear lovely Mam—

"Oi." It was Peg, kicking at Minnie's legs.
"Get up."

Gobbler, hidden up until now, growled, and
Peg backed hastily away. "Blimey! You got the
dog with you?"

Minnie grinned. "He come and found me.
Him and me, we're pals. Ain't we, Gobbler?"

Peg shook her head. "That Krick, she was
threatening to tear you into little tiny pieces –
and she didn't even know as you'd nicked the
dog. You better not go back there."

"I'd not go back for a million gold guineas,"
Minnie said fiercely. "Never!"

Sal was looking at Minnie with admiration.
"You do a lot of that? Walloping people? You did
it real good."

Unsure how to take this compliment, Minnie
squinted up at the sky.

"I reckon as we need to go this way," she
said. "Well... If you're wanting to get back to
Middleminster."

"Don't want to go any place else," Cissy told
her, but Peg looked doubtful.

"What's in it for us?" she wanted to know. "Moll and me, we was chucked out of the clothes shop. Said as we was never to darken his doors again, didn't he, Moll?"

Moll nodded. "Never again."

"We was working on a chicken farm afore we come to Middleminster," Peg went on. "Weren't too bad, but the farmer, he died, and there weren't no place for us no more."

"My Auntie Bet – she keeps chickens." Minnie smiled at the memory. "Always asking me to help. You ain't got no mam or pa, then?"

Peg shrugged. "I got an auntie somewhere, but she don't care. Got too many kids of her own to bother with the likes of me. And Moll, she come from the workhouse."

A softer look came over her face as she added, "We wouldn't mind farm work again – the two of us together."

Molly giggled. "I likes chickens."

"Never mind that," Cissy said. "We got to get going. You better keep with us for now. Come on, Min. Show us the way."

And Minnie, Gobbler close beside her, set off through the trees.

Eighteen

BY THE TIME THE SUN HAD PROPERLY risen, Minnie and her four companions had left the sheltering woods, and were well on their way. As they drew nearer to the heart of the city, the market traffic increased. Heavily laden farm carts lumbered slowly over the cobbles, and smaller one-horse traps heaped with vegetables trundled after them.

There were men wheeling barrows of cabbages or potatoes, and women carrying baskets of eggs or butter, or a couple of plucked pigeons and skinned rabbits.

Children skipped beside them, and many pithy remarks were made on the subject of the girls' yellow-and-black striped dresses. Cissy was quick to answer back, but Sal and Minnie stayed silent; Peg merely grunted, and Molly stuck out her tongue.

A clock struck seven, and Minnie wondered what lay ahead for her. She was achingly hungry, and when a small child dropped a half-eaten apple she ran to snatch it up, only to be pushed aside by the child's mother.

"Oi, you thieving hussy! Give it back."

Too tired to explain that she was starving, Minnie did as she was told.

On the other side of Middleminster, Mrs Haddington was also wide awake, and planning her day from the comfort of her silk-draped, four-poster bed.

She was enormously looking forward to visiting Haddington Hall, later that morning, and had convinced herself that she was much better off without Edith. A girl with romantic ideas was far from useful.

This afternoon, she told herself, *I shall visit dear Obadiah and tell him how well the girls have settled in*. The thought pleased her, and she smiled. *In fact, perhaps I shall go this morning, and ask if he might care to accompany me to see what joy*

a harmonious family environment can bring. It will
be a delight to be able to show him what our joint
charitable endeavours have achieved ... and perhaps
we can plan for more?

Mrs Haddington sighed happily.

What wonders might a man like that achieve with
the support of a loving wife – a wife well known for
her charitable work throughout Middleminster? Such
remarkable charitable work, too. Royal patronage
would be sure to follow...

Mrs Haddington lay back on her pillows and
closed her eyes in order to visualize this happy
future. The dream grew and grew; she was
trying to decide between a new satin gown of the
fashionable acid green or a more classic purple for
her attendance at the palace, when the rattling of
the coal scuttle disturbed her train of thought.

With regret, she returned to the activities of the
day ... and the necessity of making the scullery
maid cry.

Enry had been awake for a long time. The shed
where he slept at nights was always draughty, and
although the owner called it a stable, it hardly
deserved the name.

A ramshackle affair of old doors and planks and bits of corrugated iron, roofed with a piece of ancient canvas, it had been tossed together rather than built. The straw on the ground was clean and dry, however, and there was fresh water in the leather bucket by the door. Enry, leaning against the most reliable wall, was chewing the end of a hay stalk and discussing his future with his companion, an elderly mare.

"So, Dolly old gal – what d'you think? Seems to me like the reverend gent is as fishy as a bowl of eels. 'Got the money, has he?' That's what the strangulating fellow asked me."

Dolly blew down her nose, and Enry, taking this as encouragement, went on with his thoughts.

"So, is the Rev planning a runner? The 'New World', that fellow said – wherever that is. I needs to tell Miss Edith, and that's a fact … but how, when I can't so much as get in the door? And what's happening to Min?"

Dolly had no opinion to offer, and Enry picked up another piece of straw as an aid to constructive thought.

"Doll, I can't stand here doing nothing. I got to check on Min. But don't you worry – I'll be back, safe and sound, afore you knows it." And with that, Enry was gone.

Not thinking clearly about what he was doing, he headed towards Haddington Hall. In and out of the side streets he hurried, choosing the small back alleys in order to avoid the market traders, until he was away from the centre of the city.

The high road lay ahead, and Enry set off at a steady trot.

Sal had fallen over. A boy driving a couple of piglets to market had been so busy staring at the girls that he had failed to notice one of his small pink charges had made a dash for safety, until it was almost too late. In his frenzied dash after the squealing piglet, he knocked into Minnie, who staggered against Cissy. Cissy had only managed to stay upright by clutching at Sal, and so Sal was the one who had fallen heavily.

Now she was sitting on the muddy high road wailing loudly and clutching her ankle, and a small crowd was gathering round her.

"It's broke! My ankle's broke!" Sal glared at her sister. "That's your fault!"

"It ain't my fault – it was the pig." Cissy was unsympathetic. "You're lucky me and Min didn't fall on top of you."

The pig owner's father came to see what all the fuss was about, giving his son a clip round the ear as he passed.

Hearing Sal's wails, he bent down to look at her ankle; she gave a loud shriek of horror and tried to draw back, but he just laughed as he put out a gentle hand and felt for a broken bone.

"I'm a farrier, little Miss," he said. "I deals with horses, but a leg's a leg, and there's no break there. Maybe a twist, but nowt else."

He stood up, and moved off. Hearing the diagnosis the crowd lost interest too, and Sal was left sitting at the side of the road.

Cissy, Peg and Molly stood looking at her; it was Minnie who offered to help her, and begrudgingly Sal got to her feet. She tried a tentative step, and winced.

"Ow – I ain't never going to walk again! It hurts and hurts."

A cart heaped high with turnips was slowly grinding past and the driver, an enormous woman with her head tied up in a cheery scarlet scarf, called down, "Hurt yourself, ducky? Get up on the back!"

"Thank you!" Minnie shouted, and Peg looked at her curiously.

"Such a goody two shoes, ain't you?" she said, but it was more an observation than a criticism, and Minnie smiled at her as she helped Sal heave herself onto the back of the cart.

"Space for all," the woman said. "Up you get!"

Peg, Molly and Cissy were quick to take advantage of the invitation, but by the time the four of them were squeezed in amongst the turnips there was no room for Minnie.

The woman noticed. "Left you out, have they, ducky? You come up here with me – you and the dog," and she stretched out a ham-like arm.

A moment later Minnie and Gobbler were sitting beside their rescuer. The seat was nothing more than a rough wooden plank, and the horse was plodding along at a snail's pace, but to Minnie it was heaven. She gave a sigh of relief as she realized she could rest for a while.

The woman wasn't interested in conversation, and the cart trundled steadily on. Minnie, wedged between the warm solidity of Gobbler and the comforting bulk of the turnip owner, found herself dreaming of Mam and Bobby.

Wonder if they misses me, same as I misses them? she thought – and she sighed. Gobbler sighed in sympathy, and Minnie closed her eyes, the better to imagine what the others were doing.

She never saw Enry running towards her, and Enry only saw the four girls at the back of the cart.

Half-recognizing the yellow-and-black stripes, he halted for a moment to stare; Cissy, seeing a strange boy looking at her, made a rude gesture, and Enry shook his head and went on his way.

By the time he reached Haddington Hall a couple of hours later, Enry, remembering his run-in with Mrs Krick, had decided a cautious approach would be sensible. Carefully avoiding the front door, he slipped in between the trees like a shadow, and crept his way to the old shed at the end of the garden. The house was dark, and no smoke was rising from the chimneys; puzzled, Enry scratched his head as he took refuge in the shed. There he saw his hat hung on a nail as Minnie had left it; with a grin he put it on.

Someone found it, he thought. *Maybe it was Min?* And he looked round to see if there were any clues. His chewed turnip had been tossed into a corner, and there was a scrap of wool caught on a nail.

Enry inspected it with an eagle eye. Minnie had a red shawl...

Very cautiously, he peered out of the window to study Haddington Hall once more. There was no smoke coming from the chimneys, the windows were barred and shuttered, and he frowned.

Could they all have left? Gone somewhere else? Even as he wondered, the kitchen door opened and Mrs Krick appeared, frowsy and yawning as if she had only just woken up. She looked into the garden, clearly expecting to see something, then whistled and called, "Gobbler! Gobbler? Drat the dog: as if we ain't got enough trouble. Where's he got to?"

Enry held his breath. Was the dog roaming round in amongst the thistles? Surely he'd have seen him...

There was a muttered swear word, and the door slammed shut again. Enry relaxed a little, only to freeze a second time as Mrs Krick appeared again, this time with a young woman Enry hadn't seen before. Listening intently, he heard Mrs Krick ask her if she'd seen Gobbler.

"No, I ain't – and I ain't sorry, neither." Nellie was scowling. "I reckon he's run away, along with all the girls. Looked to me as he was sweet on Mangle: he growled at me something shocking yesterday, when I lets her out of the scullery, and he wags his tail when he sees her. Bet she's stole him."

Enry didn't wait to hear Mrs Krick's reply. He was in a state of shock. Minnie had run away? But where to?

An image of the yellow-and-black striped girls in the back of the turnip cart suddenly sprang into his mind, and he thumped his hand against the wall.

"They was from here! They was here with Min ... but she wasn't on that cart. Or was she?" He shut his eyes, trying desperately to remember what he had seen.

Had there been a flash of black and yellow at the front of the cart? Yes? No? He couldn't be sure.

I got to go and find out, he told himself, and the next minute he was heading back towards Middleminster even faster than he had come.

Nineteen

As Enry drew nearer the centre of Middleminster, the farm traffic increased. Anxiety lent speed to his weary legs, as he dodged in and out of the slow-moving vehicles, checking each one as he passed.

He had begun to worry that he had imagined the flash of black and yellow at the front of the turnip cart.

Even if he had seen something, was it Minnie? There was no real reason to think she had stayed with the other girls. And he'd assumed the cart was going to market... But what if it was going somewhere else entirely?

A cold doubt twisted inside his stomach as he passed cart after cart, and there was still no sign of her. When he finally saw the unmistakable black-and-yellow stripes ahead of him, he stopped for a second to shut his eyes.

"Let Min be there too," he murmured. "Please!" Then, opening his eyes, he ran, shouting, "Minnie? Minnie O'Sullivan … are you there?"

Minnie, meanwhile, had been fast asleep, dreaming of Mam and home. Enry's call crept into her dream, and she smiled in her sleep – then her eyes opened wide.

"ENRY?"

Enry, beaming from ear to ear, looked up at her. "I been looking for you, Min!"

With a cry of pleasure, Minnie jumped down to the road, followed by Gobbler.

She was so delighted to see Enry that she ran to hug him – but Gobbler growled loudly, and flattened his ears.

"It's all right," Minnie told him. "This here's my friend, Enry! Enry, I'm that pleased to see you, I can't say. What you doing here?"

Enry took her arm. "Following you! Min, that Miss Edith – she's trying to help you…"

He paused, as Minnie had turned to the owner of the turnip cart. She had pulled the ancient horse to a halt, and was looking at them with interest.

"Friend of yours?" she asked, and Minnie nodded.

"Thanks for the ride, Missus." She glanced up at the back of the cart; all four girls, exhausted by their early start, were deeply asleep, Molly snoring loudly. "Say goodbye to them for me when they wakes up. And… And tell Peg and Molly as my Aunt Bet could do with a hand with her chickens. Pocket Street, tell them, if you'd be so kind."

The woman nodded. "Pocket Street. I'll tell them. Stay safe, girl." With a crack of her whip, she set the cart rolling on its way once more.

Minnie watched it go.

"They wasn't always friendly to me," she said, "but they was all right in the end."

Enry grinned. "You going back to Pocket Street? Your mam – she'd be that happy to see you, she'd burst! And we got to see Miss Edith—"

Minnie shook her head sadly.

"It ain't no use Miss Edith trying to help, Enry, even though it's ever so good of her. I been thinking: I got to get away from here. Mam, she signed a paper all legal like, and if I go home they'll come and catch me and take me back. I'll be in more trouble than I ever been, because of what I did, and Enry – and I just couldn't bear it!"

Enry took her arm. "Min, you got to listen to me. That Marpike, he's up to something … and Miss Edith, she thinks so too. We been finding stuff out, Min. You got to talk to Miss Edith, honest."

Minnie looked at him in astonishment. "Up to something?"

"He's planning a runner," Enry said. "Least-ways – that's what it looks like. Min, where's the New World?"

"Right across the seas." Minnie's eyes were very round. "They told us at school."

"That's where he's going, then." Enry gave a knowing nod. "But we got to see Miss Edith. She's clever, Min, and she's trying ever so hard to get you out of trouble."

He puffed out his chest. "I knows where her house is. Come on, let's go!"

*   *   *

In Lavingley Hall, Edith had at last been let out of her room, and was now facing her mother across the breakfast table.

Lady Lavingley was complaining that Edith's shocking behaviour had kept her awake until the small hours, ruining her complexion. "If you do not wish to have an old and wrinkled mother, it is imperative that you learn to behave with decorum."

She took a sip of tea, and went on, "I have been thinking: I shall send you away. There is an excellent establishment for young ladies in Bath where you will be taught all that you currently lack in the way of manners."

Edith, aghast at this suggestion, opened her mouth to declare that the wildest of horses wouldn't drag her away from Middleminster — but the mention of Bath made her mind race in another direction.

Could this be the moment to ask about Obadiah Marpike?

She looked down at the lacy tablecloth while she collected her thoughts and then, with what she hoped was an agreeable expression, smiled at her mother.

"Whatever you say, Mother. I'm sure Bath will be a pleasant place – you spoke so well of it after your stay there."

Lady Lavingley, who had been preparing herself for the fiercest opposition, was taken off guard.

"Did I? I can't think why. It brings back nothing but the most unpleasant memories. That dreadful Sir Oliver Mothercarp! Wheedling his way into my elegant little soirées, promising that an investment in his ruby mine would bring me riches beyond my wildest dreams ... and then disappearing with my money."

"And you never met a gentleman by the name of Obadiah Marpike?" Edith held tightly to the edge of the table while she waited for the answer, and watched her mother consider the question.

"Marpike? What a curious name. No, Edith. I met no one called Obadiah Marpike. Why do you ask?"

Edith shrugged. "I heard Mrs Haddington mention someone who might have once lived there. A man of the church."

Lady Lavingley frowned. "I would prefer you not to mention that woman again, Edith.

I blame her for allowing you to leave her house unaccompanied, and I intend to write her a strongly worded letter expressing my extreme disapproval! In future, you are not to go anywhere without my permission; now, kindly ring the bell. I would like more toast."

Edith did as she was told, and then excused herself. Her mother would, without a doubt, retire from the breakfast table to her private sitting room, where she would spend the morning idly reading the gossip and scandal in the *Middleminster Daily News*. Edith's way was clear to hurry downstairs to the kitchen.

The cook greeted her favourite with a warm smile, and offered her a biscuit. "M'lady has been locking you up in your room, I hear, Miss."

She gave Edith a knowing look.

"Would that happen to have something to do with the young scallywag who came knocking at the door last night?"

"Oh: he came!" Edith sat down at the large kitchen table. "That was Enry, Mrs Mound. You didn't turn him away, did you?"

Mrs Mound shook her head. "Told him you were in your room, and you couldn't see anyone."

"Did he say he'd come back today?" Edith asked eagerly.

Mrs Mound shook her head again, and Edith's face fell.

"Oh dear … and I'm not allowed out of the house − although I'm not sure where I'd find him even if I could get out." Edith stared gloomily at the scrubbed pine table.

What if Enry didn't come back? He was her only hope of finding out about Obadiah Marpike's activities. She had guessed that he was an accomplice of the man who had swindled his way round Bath, but her mother had no recollection of meeting anybody by that name, so her guess was wrong.

A knock on the door made her look up hopefully, only to hear Mrs Mound haranguing the fishmonger's boy for being late.

I don't think Enry's going to come, she thought. *So what'll I do now?*

The fish boy was followed by an ancient knife grinder, and when he and Mrs Mound began a heated exchange about the efficiency of his scissor sharpening, Edith got up from the table to return to her room.

There's no point in sitting around and waiting, she told herself. Even as the thought passed through her mind, there was yet another knock on the door.

The kitchen maid ran to open it, and Edith, with a sudden lifting of her spirits, heard Enry's voice. She raced the kitchen maid to the door, and flung it open.

"Enry!" she said, and then, hardly able to believe her eyes, "Minnie!"

Minnie bobbed a curtsy, and grinned. "That's right, Miss. I come back like a bad penny."

There was a low growl, and Minnie looked down. "Hush, Gobbler."

Edith glanced at Mrs Mound, but she had taken her battle with the knife grinder into the scullery to demonstrate the inadequacies of his trade. Seeing that the cook was otherwise engaged, Edith pulled Enry and Minnie into the comparative quiet of the boot room, Gobbler staying close to Minnie's heels.

"I'm so pleased to see you! How did you escape from that dreadful place? Are you going home?"

A shadow crossed Minnie's face. "No, Miss. I can't do that. They'd come and find me, sure as eggs is eggs, and Mam would be in trouble, and I'd be locked up for ever and ever."

Her eyes brightened, and she gave a determined nod.

"I got a plan, though. Soon as it's dark, I'm running right away from here. There's market carts going north and south and east and west tonight. Reckon I'll hitch a ride, and—"

"No, Minnie!" Edith interrupted. "You can't do that." She settled herself on the edge of the table where the boot boy scraped clean the household's footwear. "We have to prove that Obadiah Marpike isn't what he pretends to be – and then you'll be safe."

"I found out something," Enry said eagerly, and he described Obadiah's visit to the dark and dusty shop, and Enry's conversation with the owner.

Minnie's eyes widened as she listened, and Edith gave a most unladylike whistle.

"That's so interesting," she said. "And this man talked about dirty money – and property in the New World?"

Enry nodded, and Edith whistled again. "He's planning his escape," she said. "That's what it

must be … but why? What's he escaping from?"
She bit her finger, and frowned. "Could he have
stolen something? I thought he might be working
alongside the man who swindled money out of
my mother, but she didn't know his name when
I asked her."

Minnie looked at her in surprise. "Swindled,
Miss? I thought folk like your mam knew better
than to fall for them cheaters."

Edith rolled her eyes. "Not my mother. She
met this Sir Oliver – what was his name? Oh,
yes: Mothercarp – when she was taking the
waters in Bath, and she gave him hundreds of
pounds to invest in some ruby mine or other. Of
course, he vanished, and so did her money."

Minnie and Enry were listening with intense
interest. "Funny kind of name," Enry remarked.
"Did you see him ever?"

"No," Edith said; then: "What is it, Minnie?"

Minnie had jumped to her feet. "Miss! Enry!
The swindler who tricked your mam, what if it
was the Reverend in disguise? It's all fishes, don't
you see? Carp and pike … and them first names,
they both start with an 'O', and them last names
with an 'M'!"

"'O' for 'orrible and 'M' for *misery*," Enry murmured.

Edith stared at Minnie. "Do you know – I think you might be right. That would explain why he was so upset when he heard Mother's name, wouldn't it? He was scared she'd recognize him as the man she knew in Bath. And—" her face lit up— "there's something else. Mrs Haddington talked about Obadiah investing her money in ruby mines!"

Minnie looked thoughtful. "When I upset the Reverend's table, there was a map." She screwed up her eyes to remember exactly what had happened at the Dog and Duck. "It was some other country … and all about mines, and rubies, and stuff like that."

She opened her eyes, and banged her fist on the boot box.

"Miss, it just came to me: I said I didn't know there was bust mines in other countries, and that's when he went mad and shouted at me!"

"*Bust* mines?" Edith's eyes were like saucers.

Minnie nodded. "Weren't that word, though." She struggled for a moment. "'Abandoned' … that's it. Means bust, though, don't it?"

"It certainly does." There was a pause while Edith digested Minnie's revelation. At last she said, "So now we're certain he's a rogue and a swindler, what do we do next? Should we tell the police?"

Enry looked shocked. "Word of three kids against a man like him? They'd laugh, they would. And likely as not do me and Min for lying. We needs proper proof."

"But what kind of proof?" Edith asked.

Once again, it was Minnie who had the answer. "We gets hold of that map, Miss! That *shows* as he's swindling people."

"You're right." Edith was thinking hard. "And it sounds as if he's about to do another disappearing act." She frowned. "He must be cheating Mrs Haddington, too, just like he did my mother. She collects money for her charity, and gives it to him to invest – she told me so. And now he's planning to run away with it."

Enry snorted. "Deserves all she gets, that one."

"That's true," Edith agreed. "But just think! If we could show her the map, and prove that Obadiah is a swindler, she'd be absolutely furious that she'd been tricked – and she'd want her revenge, I'm sure of it – so she'd call the police. And then he'd be thrown into jail."

She rubbed her nose thoughtfully.

"The only trouble is that she does rather hate me at the moment. We'd have to make it very clear, or she won't believe me."

"What about your mam, Miss?" Minnie asked. "She was swindled, too. What if you telled her what's going on?"

Edith considered her mother, and sighed.

"I don't think she'd believe us, even if we had a dozen maps. No: I'm sure the best way is to try and convince Mrs Haddington."

She looked at her two companions. "Are you hungry?"

"Starving, Miss." Enry's reply was heartfelt, and Minnie nodded as well.

"Ain't eaten nothing but slops since I was took to that place."

"Let's see what Mrs Mound can find," Edith said, "and then—" a resolute expression crossed her face— "we'll go out. And I'm coming too!"

Twenty

MRS HADDINGTON WAS HUMMING TO herself as her carriage drove away from the steps in front of her house and turned into Main Street.

She was mildly irritated to see that it was market day, and there were so many people crowding the narrow thoroughfare, but the thought of seeing the Reverend Obadiah Marpike kept her cheerful, and the humming continued for the duration of the journey.

On arrival at the Dog and Duck, however, the philanthropist was taken aback when she was not immediately shown to the small parlour where she and Obadiah usually met.

"The Reverend's very busy just now," the housekeeper said doubtfully. "Was he expecting you, Ma'am?"

Mrs Haddington looked down her nose. "Kindly inform him that Mrs Haddington is here to see him."

The housekeeper led her to the parlour, but ten minutes later there was still no sign of Obadiah.

What can he be doing? Mrs Haddington wondered – and then, *Such a man is sure to have many calls upon his time. I must be patient.*

Even as she made her resolve, the door opened, and Obadiah Marpike came hurrying in, apologizing profusely.

"Dear lady, dear lady – what can I say? To keep you waiting: I prostrate myself before you… I do indeed."

Mrs Haddington smiled graciously. "It is no matter."

"Oh, but it is!" There was a curious eagerness in Obadiah's tone that made Mrs Haddington look at him more closely. His fingers were covered in ink, a pen was stuck behind one ear and his pockets were full of papers.

"I do believe I have interrupted you at your labours," she said. "It is I who must apologize. I should have sent a message before arriving at your door unannounced."

Obadiah flung himself into a chair.

"No, no ... to the contrary! You could not have come at a better time."

He leant forward, and fixed his visitor with an earnest stare.

"Dear lady – do you wish to make your fortune?"

He gave a quick suspicious glance to left and right, as if fearing he might be overheard, and leant even further towards his visitor.

"I can tell no one other than you, but the most wonderful opportunity has been offered to me. All it requires is one payment of a mere thirty guineas – thirty guineas! – and we can make an investment in our ruby mine that will guarantee the most extraordinary benefits."

Mrs Haddington's mercenary heart beat faster. "Can this be true? When might we see these benefits?"

Obadiah flung out his arms. "Within six months – maybe three. My dear friend and colleague, can you join me in this venture? Thirty guineas, and the world will be yours!"

"Well ... it might be possible, Obadiah." Mrs Haddington considered her options. "I do not, of course, have such a substantial amount upon my person. I would need to return home, and write a banker's draft…"

"Excellent!" Obadiah leapt to his feet. "So might I expect the banker's draft before the end of today?"

Mrs Haddington's eyebrows rose in astonishment. "I beg your pardon?"

Obadiah realized with a jolt that he had been too eager and, fearing he was in danger of losing her support, said, "Excuse me! I was too hasty: I apologize most sincerely. My excessive enthusiasm was only caused by the urgent hope that you will join me in this venture, as my chosen companion."

Seeing Mrs Haddington's expression grow a little warmer, he added, "My chosen companion in *all* my ventures." And he raised her hand to his lips.

Mrs Haddington quivered all over. "Oh, Obadiah," she breathed, "my dear, dear man! You will always be my chosen companion. We will go through the rest of life together, and share our adventures… I accept." And she flung her arms round his neck.

This was not at all what Obadiah Marpike had intended. For a moment he resisted Mrs Haddington's all-enveloping embrace, but the rustle of papers in his pocket reminded him of his urgent need for the thirty guineas ... and promises, after all, were easily broken.

"My own sweet girl," he said. Then, wondering if this was enough, he patted her arm. "My dearest love."

It was not long after when the bride-to-be, blushing and simpering, emerged from the Dog and Duck on Obadiah's arm. The housekeeper hovered behind them; she had been informed of the forthcoming happy event, and had congratulated them with as much enthusiasm as she could muster.

"I'll be with you very shortly, dear Honoria," Obadiah promised. "I have papers to deal with, important papers that will provide for my − I should say, *our* − future together."

Mrs Haddington, blowing him a kiss and promising faithfully to send Roland with the banker's draft as soon as it could be written, climbed into her carriage and gave instructions to be driven to the orphanage. It was only as the horses turned out of Pocket Street that she remembered she had intended to tell Obadiah where she was going and to ask him to join her; the excitement of her sudden engagement had driven everything else out of her mind.

No matter, she told herself. *I shall give up the orphanage. There will be no need for it, when Obadiah and I are married.*

Obadiah, meanwhile, had gone back to his private sitting room. Papers and maps were piled everywhere, and the room had the look of belonging to someone intending to make a journey very soon. For a moment he stood still, considering the scene that had just taken place.

Marry Honoria Haddington? Never! I'd as soon marry a boa constrictor. But surely for thirty guineas I can play the part of a fond lover as long as is necessary. Chuckling to himself, he sat down at his table, and picked up a handbill advertising: *The most comfortable of journeys across the sea! The average duration of the passage across the Atlantic in our magnificent steam vessel, the S.S.* Gloriana Harrison, *is a mere seven to ten days...*

"Excellent." Obadiah glanced up at a calendar on the wall. "And five days until she's due to sail. Five days, and all this will be left behind – including—" his lip curled— "my future wife!"

His future wife was once again humming to herself, and making extravagant plans for a wedding that would be the talk of Middleminster.

Her mood was so ecstatic that she made no complaint about the slowness of the journey. She was more than happy to have time to contemplate who might usefully be invited, and how she could repay a number of small slights by leaving certain acquaintances off the guest list.

As the carriage turned into the rough road that led to Haddington Hall, she reluctantly came down to earth, and her delightful thoughts were abruptly halted as the carriage swung round and stopped in front of the orphanage.

The front door was wide open. Mrs Krick, her head swathed in bandages as if she had just that moment emerged from a tomb, was standing on the front step, wringing her hands and weeping loudly. The philanthropist, astonished by this vision, allowed her footman to open the carriage door and help her down, whereupon she was immediately assailed with an incomprehensible torrent of excuses and complaints, punctuated by loud groans.

As Mrs Haddington tried to make sense of Mrs Krick's ravings, one word caught her attention. "Gone? What do you mean, gone?" Her face turned a livid purple. "Are you telling me the girls aren't here?"

Mrs Krick clutched at her head. "Gone – but not before poor Nellie was attacked! And me thrown to the floor like a rag doll—"

"They ran away?" Mrs Haddington's anger silenced Mrs Krick for a moment. "But I pay you to guard them. Why didn't you stop them? Punish them? Lock them in?"

This remark was the trigger for such a forceful burst of swearing that Mrs Haddington took a step backwards. As she did so, Nellie emerged from the house and came to stand beside the housekeeper. When she saw her employer she too began to sob loudly, adding to the noise and confusion swirling around Mrs Haddington's ears.

"Oh, Madam, I been treated so bad… My bones is black and blue inside and out, Madam!

Them wicked girls, they beat me until I couldn't stand no more and then they was off and away. Me and Mrs Krick, we could have been dead for all they cared, madam, and they should be behind bars right now this minute."

Ten minutes before, Mrs Haddington's world had been bathed in a rosy glow. Now it was dark and threatening.

With a massive effort, she pulled herself together – and her expression was not pleasant.

"I am astonished and distressed by your lack of efficiency," she said. "When I return home, I will see that each of you is paid the equivalent of one week's wages, but not a penny more ... and if I hear another word from either of you, I shall send you straight to the courts for insubordination and inadequate service. I can assure you that I will be believed over any ridiculous claims you might make."

With one final glare at Mrs Krick and Nellie, Mrs Haddington climbed back into her carriage.

"To the Dog and Duck!" she ordered. "As quickly as you can."

The coachman nodded, and picked up his whip ... and Mrs Haddington began the journey back to the city. As the carriage jolted along the road, her anger cooled a little.

After all, I was thinking of closing down my charitable work, she thought. *Those four girls are no real loss; they can take their chances. But my dear Obadiah was so concerned that Mangle should be kept within the walls – what will he say when I tell him she has escaped?* She frowned. *She must be found. Found, and properly punished. Obadiah was too generous; he should have immediately brought her before the law.*

Mrs Haddington nodded as she made a decision.

I shall report her assault to the police, and have a warrant put out for her arrest. In fact, I shall call in at the police station on my way to the Dog and Duck in order to set the process in motion. An officer of the law must accompany me, in order that my fiancé— Mrs Haddington fluttered and blushed as she allowed herself the word— *can give him a first-hand account.*

And she glowed in anticipation of Obadiah's admiration and gratitude, as she tapped on the roof of the carriage to attract the driver's attention.

Twenty-one

WHILE ENRY AND MINNIE TUCKED INTO quantities of bread, cheese and large slices of apple pie, and Gobbler chewed happily on a meaty bone, Edith made her plan of escape.

I can't go out the front door, she told herself. *I'll have to find another way... Oh, bother these skirts!*

Another thought came to her, and she gave a little gasp.

Of course: I'll dress as a boy — that's what girls always do in stories. I can borrow Father's clothes.

Waiting until Enry and Minnie had eaten as much as they wanted, and smiling as Mrs Mound clucked over their pale faces like an over-anxious mother hen, Edith led her friends to the door.

"I'll say goodbye," she said loudly, "and thank you for all your help." Then, as Enry opened the door, she breathed, "Wait for me round the corner. I'll meet you there in – oh, ten minutes."

Minnie, catching her intention, called a cheery, "Goodbye, Miss, and ta for the vittles!" as the door shut behind her and Enry.

"Thank you so much." Edith flung her arms round the cook. "Thank you for giving them the food, and the dog, too!"

Mrs Mound looked pleased. "There, there. What's a bite or two of bread and cheese, and an old bone? Now, you run along and stop cluttering up my kitchen."

Whisking up the stairs, Edith saw her mother's sitting room door was open, and peeped inside. Lady Lavingley was asleep on her day bed with her mouth open; newspapers were strewn on the floor, and a large box of sweetmeats was on the table beside her.

Much relieved, Edith tiptoed on to her father's room. Opening the door, she wasn't entirely surprised to see that dust lay heavily on every surface. Lady Lavingley had never been an overly fond or caring wife; when Colonel Lavingley was killed at the Battle of Khartoum, Edith's mother had worn the necessary black, closed up his bedroom and devoted herself with enthusiasm to her own interests and pleasures.

Edith moved as silently as she could to the heavy mahogany wardrobe – scanning the contents, she chose a pair of black trousers, a shirt, a waistcoat and a bowler hat.

Bundling these up, she hurried along the corridor to her bedroom, hoping against hope that she wouldn't meet any of the servants. She was in luck: the bedrooms had already been cleaned and swept, and her way was clear.

Ten minutes later, a strange-looking figure crept down the back stairs. Colonel Lavingley had been a slender man and Edith found his clothes fitted her well, but the excessive length of the trousers had caused her problems. Scissors had been necessary; Edith had felt a momentary pang as she hacked ten inches from the trouser legs, but had reassured herself that it was for an excellent cause.

Father went to war to fight for what's right, she thought, *and that's what I'm doing now.*

The bowler hat was also much too large, so the trouser ends had been useful as stuffing before she scooped up her hair and rammed the hat well down over her forehead.

Now, tiptoeing down the corridor that led to the servants' hall, she looked to left and right before dashing for the side door that opened onto the courtyard.

She was so intent on escape that she failed to hear the footsteps behind her; her fingers were on the door handle when a heavy hand grabbed the back of her waistcoat and spun her round.

"Oh no you don't, you young scallywag—"

"Harbottle!" Edith gasped, but her shock was nothing compared to that of the butler, whose mouth was hanging open like a goldfish.

"Miss Edith?"

"Yes, it's me." Desperation and determination made Edith clench her fists. "And, Harbottle, if you ever, *ever* cared for my father, you've got to let me go out."

Harbottle blinked. "But—"

"If you don't let me, I... I'll tell Mother that you put water in the whisky!" Edith's eyes flashed.

The butler went scarlet. "That's a big fat fib, Miss Edith. If your father could hear you, he'd be ashamed of you – accusing an honest man."

"But that's exactly what's happened to my friend!" Edith grabbed Harbottle's sleeve. "She's been accused of something she didn't do, and I've got to help her − *please,* Harbottle."

A curious expression crossed the butler's face, and he said, "Never saw it before, Miss Edith … but you're the spit of your father. I'll let you go, but—" he stopped Edith's thanks with an upheld hand— "on condition that you inform me of your destination, and your companions."

"The Dog and Duck."

Edith reached up and, to his astonishment, kissed the butler's weather-worn old cheek.

"And I'm going with Enry and Minnie … and thank you!"

And then she was gone. Slipping out of the door, she hurried over the cobbles of the stable yard, ignoring a shout from one of the grooms.

A moment later she was out in the street, and running to meet her fellow conspirators.

"I'm here!" she called, "I'm here!"

Enry and Minnie swung round − and stared. Gobbler, less easily deceived, wagged his tail.

"Cripes: is that really you, Miss?" Enry sounded disbelieving, and Edith grinned.

"You'd better call me … um … Frederick," she said.

Minnie giggled. "Freddie," she suggested. "Frederick sounds like a right proper toff."

"Freddie," Edith agreed. "And I've not got a lot of time, so let's go – and we need to think of a way to get that map. We absolutely must search Obadiah's room."

Enry nodded. "Me and Min, we was just talking about that."

"We got to get him out of the way," said Minnie, "so I says, why don't Enry tell him as your Mrs Haddington wants him at her place?"

"I been to her house before." Enry pointed out. "So it makes sense that I got to take another message." He gave Edith a hopeful look. "We thought you could tell us something like what she'd say?"

"Of course!" Edith brightened, then was cast down again. "But I haven't got any paper, or pens or ink to write on."

"Don't need none," Minnie told her. "Enry just needs the right words … but if you wants to write it out, I got paper."

She pulled a scrap of paper bag from her pocket, and Enry produced the stub end of a much-chewed pencil.

Edith took them, and as they hurried together along the street, she tried to think of the best way to coax Obadiah out of his lair. *What does he care about most?* she wondered, and then, remembering Mrs Haddington's tea party and that lady's attempts to attract contributions, she stopped for a moment. "Of course: money. If he thinks Mrs Haddington has money for him, he's bound to go and see her."

Enry nodded, but Minnie was thoughtful. "What if you just says it's ever such good news, Miss – I means, Freddie! Good news as she wants to tell him in person. Folks get ever so curious when they hears about a mystery."

Edith looked at Minnie with genuine admiration. "You're right: I'd want to know what the mystery was." And then, leaning on a convenient postbox, she began to write: *Mrs Haddington's compliments to the Reverend Obadiah Marpike. She is in the possession of some excellent news that will be much to the advantage of their mutual cause, and wishes to inform him in person. She would be most grateful if he could call at the very earliest opportunity.* It was the others' turn to look admiring as she read her composition out loud, and when she was finished, Edith beamed. "Let's hope it works! Enry ... can you read my writing?"

"Don't need to. I takes lots of messages," Enry told her, and he repeated it word for word.

Edith shook her head in wonder. "I wish I had a memory like yours."

She took Minnie's arm.

"Come on. Let's go and lay our trap!"

Twenty-two

OBADIAH MARPIKE WAS STRIDING UP AND down his room, biting his lip. Mrs Haddington's banker's draft for thirty guineas had still not arrived, and although he was almost certain that she intend＿ ＿ ＿ ＿ ＿ ＿ nise, there was just enough ＿ ＿ ＿ ＿ ＿ ＿ ke him anxious.

"Sh＿ ＿ ＿ ＿ ＿ at, M＿ ＿ ＿ ＿ ＿ smiled a crocodile smile. ＿ ＿ ＿ up a＿ ＿ mano＿ I suppose I might be forgi＿ ＿ s right. A ＿ ＿ e my beloved … but I have ＿ ＿ iously at ＿ ＿ her suspicions—" A knock on ＿ ＿ ＿ companion ＿ ＿ n stop. "Yes?"

The house＿ ＿ ＿ ＿ ＿ ＿ and then curtsyed. "If you please, S＿ ＿ ＿ ＿ ＿ e with a message for you. He says it's from Mrs Haddington."

"Send the boy in at once," Obadiah ordered. "I was expecting to hear from her."

The housekeeper bobbed another curtsy, and turned towards the door. "Enry, come in!"

Enry, who had been worrying that Obadiah would suspect that his message wasn't genuine, was pleasantly surprised by the eagerness with which the reverend gentleman greeted him.

"Yes? I was expecting to hear from Mrs Haddington – what is it?"

Holding his thumbs behind his back for luck, Enry carefully repeated Edith's words, and saw Obadiah's face brighten.

"Excellent: run back and say I will be there immediately." Obadiah snatched up his coat, stick and hat. "What a꞉ ⬛ ꞉en? Run, boy – run!"

And as Enry, ⬛ grin, slid out of the room꞉⬛ ꞉ close behind him.

Minnie and Edith ⬛ ꞉e Dog and Duck, saw Enry co⬛

To their surpris꞉ ⬛ knowledge them, but the reason becan⬛obvious as Obadiah emerged shortly after, and strode towards the cab rank at the end of the road – where an ancient horse was drooping over his nosebag, and his driver was eating a hunk of cheese.

"Garston Street, and be quick about it." And then he was inside the cab, slamming the door behind him.

Edith looked at Minnie, her eyes alight with excitement. "That's where Mrs Haddington lives… He's gone!"

"So now we've got to get in," Minnie said, and she gave the Dog and Duck a considering stare. "That there's the Reverend's window. When we come here to see him, Enry, he peeked in there to see what he were up to."

"So will we climb in?" Edith was already on the move, and Minnie caught her arm.

"Can't do that. Look … there's all kinds of folk walking down."

Minnie was right. Already a few passers-by had looked curiously at the boy in the bowler hat, his shabby companion, and the large hairy dog, and it was obvious that any activity that looked suspicious would be noticed.

There was the sound of flying feet, and Enry arrived back beside them, red-faced and panting. "I had to go round the block," he explained.

"Couldn't risk him catching sight of me." He wiped his forehead, and took a deep breath. "Blimey: I'm all puffed out."

"Enry!" Minnie clapped her hands. "I got an idea. Freddie here—" she twinkled at Edith— "wants to climb in the window, but I says we'd have the police down on us, sure as donkeys bray. But if you goes puffing in, you can say as the Reverend's forgot his papers, and next thing you'll be shown to his room, easy as pie!"

"Cripes." Enry stared at her. "You don't half have a lot of good ideas, our Min. So, where does I look for the map?"

"He knocked it off the table," Minnie said. "Dunno if he put it back there, though."

"I'll find it," Enry promised, and then he was gone.

Having already seen Obadiah hurry away in response to Enry's message, it was easy for the housekeeper to accept the boy's story. He found himself in Obadiah's private sitting room without any questions asked, but he was accompanied to the doorway, and the housekeeper showed no sign of leaving.

Flustered, Enry looked round at the heaps of newspapers, bills, letters and ledgers.

"He says it were the papers on the table," he said, "but he never said which ones. Picture of a map – and something about ruby mines...?"

The housekeeper didn't answer. She was looking round the room; noticing the half-packed bags and cases, an unpleasant idea crept into her mind.

He owes me four guineas, she thought, and her mouth tightened. *If he's planning a moonlight flit, he'll have me to reckon with!*

But then, remembering Obadiah's engagement, she relaxed again.

A wedding trip, perhaps. And then I suppose he'll move into that woman's house. No loss – as long as he pays his debts. I'll advertise for a nice, quiet gentlewoman, that's what I'll do.

While the housekeeper was musing over Obadiah's intentions, Enry was sifting through his papers. He could see nothing that concerned mines, or rubies – although there did seem to be a remarkable number of unpaid bills.

As a last resort he moved a couple of books, and in so doing knocked a heap of papers and documents onto the floor.

The housekeeper frowned. "Pick those up at once, Enry! Didn't the Reverend tell you where to look? He'll not be happy when he sees this mess." She shook her head. "Find what he sent you for, and get out of here. I can hear wheels; that'll be a customer – unless it's the Reverend coming back to get his documents for himself."

Enry's hands were trembling as he gathered up the scattered papers, doing his best to check them as he did so. There was still no sign of a map; his stomach was beginning to swirl unpleasantly as he wondered what he should do next. Minnie was relying on him...

As the thought of Minnie crossed his mind, there was a sudden outraged scream from outside: a scream followed by shouts, cries and furious barking. Enry and the housekeeper flew to the window, and Enry's heart sank into his over-large boots.

An enormous policeman was standing outside; Minnie's arm was firmly held by one enormous hand, and Gobbler, twisting and wriggling and snapping wildly at the air was suspended by the other. There was no sign of Edith ... but Mrs Haddington was standing watching, with an exultant smile.

Twenty-three

MINNIE, SITTING ON A LOW STOOL IN THE parlour of the Dog and Duck, was very pale.

The policeman was close beside her, although, despite Mrs Haddington's urgent instructions, Police Constable Gubbs had refused to handcuff Minnie until Obadiah had laid a formal charge of assault. The philanthropist had not endeared herself to him; she had been arrogant and overbearing, and the policeman's sympathies were with Minnie rather than her accuser.

Her hands folded in her lap and her eyes cast down, Minnie looked defeated ... but her thoughts were racing. It was Gobbler's fault that she and Edith had been distracted from watching the road: a young man and his dog had been walking by, and the dog had issued a challenge to Gobbler – and Gobbler had retaliated by launching himself at the challenger with a flurry of growls and barks.

It had taken both Minnie and Edith to pull him away, and in the confusion neither of them had heard the carriage approaching until it was too late. The policeman had leapt out and, instructed by screams from Mrs Haddington, captured both Minnie and Gobbler.

Edith, aghast, had agonized for a second – should she stay, or should she run? Minnie, held firm by the arm of the law, had seen her face.

"Run, Freddie!"

And Edith had vanished.

Now, staring at the floor, Minnie was wondering where Edith had gone.

She'll be thinking of something from one of them books of hers, Minnie told herself, and the thought gave her a faint glimmer of hope. *And Enry … what's he doing? Saw him come dashing out – but I never saw what he did then.*

She was unable to repress a sigh.

I guess he ain't found the map – so what'll happen now?

* * *

Outside, Edith had emerged from hiding as soon as Minnie had been escorted into the inn, and found a miserable Gobbler tied to the railings with a piece of rope. Enry was standing near him, looking just as forlorn.

"Did you find the map?" Edith asked urgently, and Enry shook his head.

"Weren't no sign," he said, and Edith groaned.

"So what are we going to do?" she said – and then, "we've got to get Minnie out of there."

Enry was still drooping. "I don't see how, Miss. That copper got her, and he ain't likely to let her go."

Edith rubbed her nose. "What if we make a distraction? So the policeman thinks there's something even more important, and comes running out?"

"A what, Miss?" Enry looked blank.

"If we make a terrible noise, or something." Edith shut her eyes to think better. "A robbery! That would do... A young lady passing by has been attacked and robbed. In the stories, the hero always rushes to help a lady in distress – so a policeman certainly ought to. It's his job."

"If you say so, Miss."

Enry was willing to agree to anything that might help Minnie, unlikely as Edith's plan might be.

"But where'll we get the lady from?"

Edith opened her eyes. "Me. I'll scream."

Enry brightened. "You might be onto something, Miss. There's a back door to the Dog. If you can get the copper out here, I can slip in that way and find Min..." He paused. "What about the old woman?"

"Mrs Haddington?" Edith rubbed her nose again. "Won't she come running out with the policeman?"

"Worth a try," Enry said.

"That's all we can do." Edith was determined to believe in her plan. "I'd better make sure I can't be seen from the window. Are you ready, Enry?"

"Give me a couple of minutes," Enry said. "I got to get in, and that back door sticks."

Edith nodded, and Enry shot away round the corner.

A moment later he was easing the back door open. It led into a narrow corridor, and he crept his way along, hardly daring to breathe.

Just before the parlour, the corridor took a sudden turn, providing him with cover; if he peered round, he could see the parlour door and the wider passage beyond that led to the main front door.

Crossing his fingers, he waited.

Mrs Haddington, seated across the room from Minnie and PC Gubbs, was mentally congratulating herself. Her capture of the girl had, she considered, been a triumph, and she was waiting eagerly for Obadiah to return so that she could present him with her prisoner.

A glance at Minnie's bent head made her smile — the girl was, at last, subdued. And once Obadiah had reported the details of Minnie's attack, she intended to stand beside him and watch Minnie being taken away. Justice would finally be done, and he would be eternally grateful; she gave a small sigh of pleasurable anticipation at the thought.

And then we will live happily ever after, she told herself.

"Thief! Thief! Help! Oh — somebody please help me!"

The scream was piercing, and was immediately followed by ferocious barking.

"Help! My purse! Help me!"

"What's that?" PC Gubbs leapt to his feet and ran to the window. "Can't see nothing from here—" and then, just as Edith had predicted, he rushed out of the room, leaving Mrs Haddington open-mouthed and staring.

Before the philanthropist could move, Minnie too was up, and hurtling towards the door. Mrs Haddington, purple with rage, rose from her chair in an effort to stop her – but Minnie was gone.

The door was slammed shut … and there was the unpleasant grating sound of a key turning in the lock.

On the other side, Enry grinned. "That'll keep her quiet," he said.

But Minnie didn't hear him; she was already tearing down the corridor to Obadiah's room, with just one thing on her mind.

"I got to find it! I ain't going to prison – I ain't, I ain't!"

Praying that the door was unlocked, she lifted the latch … and found herself inside.

There were piles of paper everywhere. On the table, on the chairs and on the floor. Minnie, her heart racing, took a deep breath, and made herself look slowly round.

"It was with other papers, all with a big crest," she told herself. "And it'll have ink on it…"

A pile under the table caught her eye, and she bent down to look more closely.

Yes! There were ink stains splattered over the crabbed and crooked writing. Ink stains – but no crest.

She moved the pile to one side … and there was another heap of ink-stained papers underneath.

Hands trembling, she fluttered the papers this way and that – and there, right in front of her, was the map.

With a triumphant cry, she snatched it up, and looked round for Enry … and Enry was there, but he wasn't alone.

Beside him was Edith, and the solid form of PC Gubbs, his heavy hand on Edith's shoulder.

Minnie blinked – and launched herself at the policeman before he could say a word.

"Mister, Mister! See this map? I got to show it to her – to that Mrs Haddington. You can clap me in irons or whatever you want – but I absolutely *got* to show her!"

PC Gubbs' eyebrows rose to the level of his helmet, but all he said was, "You come along of me, Miss. Back to where you was, and I'll thank these lads to come, too."

He gave Edith a thoughtful glance.

"I caught this here young fellow distracting an officer during the execution of his duty, and he tells me he's a pal of yours. We needs to talk things over, seems to me."

Twenty-four

MRS HADDINGTON WAS IN A TOWERING rage. When PC Gubbs unlocked the door and ushered Minnie, Edith and Enry back into the parlour, she rushed at Minnie, hands outstretched to grab at her.

"Evil, evil girl!" she screeched, but she was stopped by the substantial arm of PC Gubbs.

"That's enough, Ma'am – we'll have no fisticuffs, if you please."

Eyes bulging, and quivering with rage, Mrs Haddington retired to her chair. "Officer, I insist the girl is handcuffed! You saw how she tried to escape. Do your duty... Do it NOW."

PC Gubbs shook his head firmly. "The young person assures me she'll stay right here."

"And you believe her?"

Seething, Mrs Haddington tried again.

"She's nothing more than a lying gutter-snipe—"

"I ain't none of that! But you – you're a silly old woman who's being swindled good and proper." Minnie was raging. "You're being rooked, you are. There ain't no ruby mines! Bet you was promised gold and all sorts ... but none of it's true."

And she waved the map under Mrs Haddington's outraged nose.

"See? See what it says? 'Abandoned'. And the Reverend – he's running off, and he's taking all your money with him! Took you for a ride on the roundabout horses, and now he's got what he wants, he's going to dump you. His boxes and bags is packed, all ready for a flit... Go and see. He's the liar – not me!"

Mrs Haddington went pale, then red, then pale again as she studied the map.

"I don't believe you," she said at last. "My Obadiah is an honourable man. There will be an explanation for this, without a doubt."

"He's not honourable!" Edith stepped forward. "Minnie's right – he's a cheat and a swindler and a liar. He lied about Minnie attacking him. I know he did ... didn't he, Enry?"

Enry nodded. "He ain't any good, and that's the gospel truth."

PC Gubbs, a solid rock in the middle of a choppy ocean, intervened.

"Seems to me as there's a lot of accusations going on here," he remarked. "And all about this reverend gent. What I suggests is, we wait here and let him speak for himself." He looked at Mrs Haddington. "Would that be agreeable to you, Ma'am?"

Mrs Haddington had taken the time to gather herself together.

"It certainly would, Officer. As soon as the Reverend Obadiah Marpike walks through that door, you will see that you have been hoodwinked by this ... this rabble!"

She gave the map a defiant glare.

"This proves nothing. Nothing at all!"

The Reverend Obadiah Marpike was mystified. Arriving at Honoria Haddington's house, he had been informed that the lady had gone out in her carriage some while before.

"Are you certain that no message was left for me?" he had asked, over and over again.

"No, Sir." The maid had been emphatic. "There's no message. I'd be sure to tell you if there was."

There was nothing else for Obadiah to do but leave his card, and return home. He strode through the streets in a state of agitation; what was Honoria playing at?

It wasn't long before it occurred to him that someone else might have sent the message. The wording had been such that he never suspected Enry; as he searched his mind for possibilities, he grew increasingly alarmed.

It must be someone who knows of my connection with Honoria ... but who could that be? An unpleasant suspicion came to him, and he began to mutter out loud.

"They wanted me away from the Dog – they wanted me to leave – but why? What are they after? I must get back at once!"

And, seeing no cab close to hand, he broke into a run.

Startled passers-by stared as he dashed past, wild-eyed, and the unfortunate basket seller who blocked his way was sent sprawling, his baskets scattered.

On and on Obadiah ran until he was in sight of the Dog and Duck – and there, at last, he stopped, panting.

A familiar coach was standing in the gateway; as he looked at it, his doubts and concerns faded.

That foolish maid was mistaken, he told himself as he recovered his breath. *Honoria must have tired of waiting for me, and made her way here. Let us hope she brought the banker's draft!*

As he strode into the Dog and Duck, the housekeeper came hurrying out to meet him. "You're wanted in the parlour, Sir," she said, and Obadiah's mood lifted.

"Mrs Haddington is there?"

"Yes, Sir."

The housekeeper was fighting her conscience. Should she warn her lodger that there was also a policeman? With a shrug, she decided there was no reason to mention it, and retreated to the safety of her kitchen.

Obadiah, unsuspecting, opened the parlour door. Before he could say a word, his affianced bride had thrown herself into his arms.

"Obadiah, my dearest − the moment has come at last! An officer of the law is waiting to hear you accuse Minnie O'Sullivan, so that justice can finally be done. Tell the officer to charge her, Obadiah!"

Obadiah's response was not at all what his beloved had expected. He froze, and Mrs Haddington, pressed against his chest, heard him hiss, "You stupid, stupid woman ... do you know what you've done?"

Astonished, she pushed him away. "Obadiah?"

"Ask him about them rubies!" Minnie had seen Mrs Haddington's discomfiture. "Ask him." She thrust the map under Obadiah's nose.

As Obadiah tried to calm his whirling thoughts, a thunderous knocking made everyone jump. The next minute heavy footsteps came marching towards the parlour door, and it was flung open to reveal—

"Harbottle!" Edith's eyes grew very round ... and then she saw the figure standing behind the butler. "MOTHER!"

But her mother wasn't looking at her. She was staring at Obadiah Marpike as if she was seeing a ghost.

"You! SIR OLIVER MOTHERCARP – TELL ME … WHERE IS MY MONEY?"

As every eye turned to Obadiah, he swore loudly and made a dash for the door – but PC Gubbs was faster. In three strides he had the swindler by the arm, and a moment later the handcuffs were on his wrists.

With a grunt of satisfaction, the policeman inspected his prisoner.

"So *you're* 'Sir Oliver Mothercarp'… Well, I never. We've been on the lookout for you for a long time now. Never knew as you were on the doorstep, so to speak – last heard of you in Bath – but here you are, and here you'll stay for a good long stretch."

Mrs Haddington was looking from Lady Lavingley to Edith, and back again. Her voice quavered as she asked, "You know this man?"

"Know him?" Lady Lavingley looked down her nose. "My good woman, he swindled me out of hundreds of pounds. Some taradiddle about a ruby mine, and I was foolish enough to believe him."

She looked at PC Gubbs.

"I trust he will be placed behind bars."

"Ho, yes." The policeman puffed out his chest. "Wanted in Bath, Canterbury and Wells, he is. There's a reward of a hundred pound … that's how much he's wanted."

Edith jumped forward. "Then Minnie should have it! That horrible man had her sent to the Haddington Hall, because she'd seen the map of the ruby mine – and he was scared she'd tell people it was abandoned. If it hadn't been for *that*, we'd none of us be here."

Lady Lavingley was staring at Edith. "Edith?" She blinked, and looked again. "Edith … is that you?"

Edith pulled off her hat, and her hair tumbled round her shoulders. "Yes, Mother."

Her mother put her hand to her throat, and sank onto a chair. "Edith – Edith – *what* have you been doing?"

It was Minnie who answered. "Your Miss Edith, she's a hero, Missus. She and Enry here, they been helping me. You did ought to be really proud of her, Missus. Really proud."

Lady Lavingley, who had never in her entire life been instructed in how she should feel, looked helplessly at PC Gubbs, who nodded.

"Seems like all three of them have been working together. Right little team."

"I see." With an effort, Edith's mother stood up again, and when she spoke she was clearly choosing her words with care. "Edith, it would appear that you have helped to apprehend a criminal – a criminal who caused me much distress. For that reason, I am prepared to overlook the extremely curious way in which you have been behaving, and the extraordinary garments in which you are dressed. We will put it behind us, and move on. My carriage is outside. Let us go."

But Edith shook her head. "I'm sorry, Mother. I want to make sure Minnie gets home safely. She's my friend … and so is Enry."

Lady Lavingley stood very still, trying to make a decision. Could it be that she might make something positive out of what had happened? A daughter who had been instrumental in bringing her mother's persecutor to justice? That would be very different – and surely it would be considered admirable.

She made her choice. "Edith, you may see your friends home. Harbottle, you will arrange for the carriage to collect Miss Edith whenever she wishes."

She gave Enry and Minnie a considering glance.

"And they may visit. If they wish, of course." And then, unable to completely give up her prejudices, she added, "It would be best to receive them in the kitchen."

It was at that moment that Lady Lavingley had the surprise of her life – Edith ran to her, and hugged her.

"Thank you! Oh, thank you, Mother!"

Minnie, Edith and Enry stood and watched as PC Gubbs and a scowling Obadiah left the Dog and Duck. The housekeeper came to join them for a moment before shaking her head and going back to her kitchen.

"Took me in good and proper," she said to herself, and soothed her feelings by retreating to her kitchen and writing out an advertisement for a lady lodger.

Mrs Haddington scuttled to her carriage without a word. As she passed Minnie, she gave her a look of such intense venom that Edith gasped, but Minnie shook her head as if she was almost sorry for her persecutor.

"She ain't worth nothing, that one," she said. "And she ain't *got* nothing now, neither. Look at her now. She's lost it all, and she knows it."

Enry grinned. "Got what she deserves, and that's a fact."

Lady Lavingley was the last to leave the Dog and Duck, accompanied by Harbottle, who winked at Edith after helping her mother settle in amongst her cushions. Edith smiled back.

"Harbottle ... what made my mother come here?" she asked. "I've been wondering."

"She got to thinking about what you'd been up to," the butler said. "Asked me to call you, but I could hardly do that... And when she found out you were missing – why, a right carry on, it was. Weeping and wailing, and saying she'd been too harsh with you..."

"Really?" Edith felt a warm glow.

Harbottle nodded. "So I had to tell her where you were."

For the second time that day Edith kissed him. "Thank you."

"Harbottle?" Lady Lavingley's tone was imperious. "I'm waiting!"

The butler grinned. "See you later, Miss Edith."

As the carriage rolled away, Minnie took Edith's hand. "They come in all shapes and sizes, mams do. And now—" she swallowed a sob— "I wants to see my mam and Bobby. I wants to see them something dreadful!"

Twenty-five

As Minnie, Edith, Gobbler and Enry hurried along Pocket Street, Edith and Enry drew back a little, thinking Minnie would want to greet her mother and little brother alone. Minnie, however, had no such thoughts; looking over her shoulder, she told them to hurry up.

"You got to meet my mam! You got to meet our Bobby!"

Enry and Edith did as they were told. Once they were in Pocket Yard, however, Minnie stopped, and turned to Enry.

"You knock." Her face was shining. "Tell her as you've got a surprise!"

Grinning, Enry knocked as Minnie drew Edith to one side. The door opened, and Edith saw a mountain of a woman with sad eyes and

drooping shoulders step out. A small boy with
curly hair was close beside her, his thumb in his
mouth.

"Enry! What you doing here?" Her voice was
dull, but Bobby looked hopefully at Enry.

"You seen our Min?"

Enry opened his mouth to give his message,
but Minnie couldn't wait.

With a loud cry of "Mam!" she hurled herself
into her mother's arms.

"Min!"

Bobby clutched his sister's legs and Minnie,
tears running down her cheeks, scooped him up
and hugged him so tightly that he squealed.

Gobbler, aware that something wonderful
was happening, ran round and round in circles,
barking ecstatically until Minnie finally let Mam
and Bobby go, and hushed him.

"Lovely, ain't it?" Enry, too, had tears in
his eyes.

Edith nodded. "Should we leave them, do you
think?"

But Minnie was already looking round for
them. Seizing their hands, she pulled them
forward.

"Mam! Mam! This here's Edith, and she and Enry – they was the ones as rescued me."

Mam O'Sullivan looked from one to the other. "I'm all of a whirl. You better come in." She shook her head. "Don't know as I've ever been so knocked all of a heap." A sudden thought made her turn to Minnie. "You ain't got the police looking for you, have you, Min?"

Minnie laughed. "No. Free as a bird, me."

Bobby was looking at her dress. "Funny clothes. All yellow and black."

Minnie smiled at him. "You'll never see it again, Bobs."

She pulled up a chair for Edith, and she and Enry settled themselves on the edge of her mam's bed.

"You ready to hear it all, Mam?"

And Mam O'Sullivan, glowing with happiness, sat herself down to listen.

It was the day after Minnie's return, when Peg and Molly came walking down Pocket Street. Minnie was on her way to visit Aunt Bet when Gobbler started alternately growling and wagging his tail, and Minnie looked up to see the girls shifting from foot to foot with anxious expressions. They were still wearing their yellow-and-black dresses, and it was obvious that they had slept in them the night before, and that their resting place had been wet and muddy.

Minnie, overcome with pity, smiled at them, and they smiled back, pleased to find she wasn't annoyed to see them.

"Come to find you," Peg said, and she sounded unusually hesitant. "Cissy and Sal – they got back with their gran. Ever so glad to have them back, she was. But us, we ain't got nowhere. And that carter – she said as you said something about chickens…"

Molly nodded. "I likes chickens."

Minnie's smile widened. "I'm on my way to Aunt Bet's right now. She needs a bit of help – she'd like to sell eggs, but she don't have the time."

For the first time since Minnie had met her, Molly spoke without echoing Peg. "Ta, Minnie. You're a good girl, you is."

In the course of time, the courts released what was left of Obadiah Marpike's ill-gotten gains, and although Lady Lavingley never received all the money she had lost, she was content with what she had. She treated Edith with a mixture of admiration and respect, and Edith was allowed to come and go as she pleased – often with Enry as her escort.

Remembering his remarkable memory, Edith persuaded her mother to pay for Enry to go to school ... and he proved to be easily the most able pupil in the class.

Mrs Haddington? She retired from public life. Edith told Minnie that she thought she had seen her behind a stall at a charity market, but she looked so different – so worn and haggard – that she couldn't be certain.

"Never mind," Minnie said cheerfully when she heard. "I ain't bothered about her no more."

Best of all, Minnie did get the reward of a hundred pounds. She tried hard to share it with Edith and Enry, but they both refused her offer, and in the end she gave up trying.

Instead, she made sure that the little stone cottage she bought for Mam, Bobby and herself had an extra room ... a room with *ENRY* written on the door.

Outside the cottage was a garden big enough for several rows of vegetables, a nanny goat and a flower bed – and Minnie never had to turn the mangle again.

VIVIAN FRENCH has written more than 300 books for children. Her recent work includes a junior fiction series with Marta Kissi: *The Adventures of Alfie Onion*, *The Cherry Pie Princess*, *Tom & Tallulah and the Witches' Feast*, *The Dragon's Breakfast*, and *The Giants' Tea Party* – and the critically acclaimed picture book *The Most Wonderful Thing in the World*, with artwork by Angela Barrett. Vivian teaches at Edinburgh College of Art and can be seen at festivals all over the country. She helped to found the mentoring scheme Picture Hooks for aspiring young illustrators, and was awarded the MBE for services to literature, literacy, illustration and the arts.

Follow Vivian on Twitter under the handle @fivekingdoms, or visit her at her website: **www.vivianfrench.com**